I0552237

Race the Wind

Children of the Wild, Volume 6

Prudence MacLeod

Published by Prudence MacLeod, 2024.

RACE THE WIND

First edition. March 6, 2024.

ISBN: 978-1927478691

Written by Prudence MacLeod.

Race the Wind

By
Prudence MacLeod
(second edition)

Copyright November 9th/2017
All Rights Reserved

Premonition

The queen of the vampires awakened with a start, breathing deeply as she tried to shake off the spell of the vision. "Sally, my beloved, what is it?" Concerned, the king took her gently into his arms. "Hush now, I've got you, you're safe. Tell me what you saw."

She snuggled against him, retreating into the protection of his arms. "I saw a time of danger, Harald, danger of discovery. Somehow, a horse is at the center of it, but it's Igor and Rhonda who are the key."

"Igor and Rhonda?"

"Yes, if they can't hold true to each other, all will be lost. If they can, we have a solid chance, but it's the horse that will make or break it."

"So what do we do?"

"Nothing, Harald, my love. There's nothing we can do. It's going to be up to the Hawk and the Wolf; our future lies in their hands, their ability to function, the strength of their love for each other. This will be their greatest test, and all our fates hang in the balance.

"Harald, we can't let them know. We can't tell a single soul until it's over. We just have to believe in them and trust them to prove true to each other."

He hugged her shoulders gently then sighed. "Well, both hawks and wolves mate for life, that much is in our favor. Is there nothing at all we can do?"

"We can help them if they ask, no more. Harald, you poor man, it must be torture being married to a psychic."

With a chuckle, he hugged her again. "Actually, I quite like it, and being forewarned before danger arrives is never a bad thing. Do you know what the danger is?"

"Exposure to the public."

He sighed again. "Damn."

Wild Horses

"Goddammit, them wild horses broke through our fence again." The angry man threw his hat on the ground, swore as he kicked the tire on his jeep, then snatched up the hat and beat the dust off it against the thigh of his jeans. "That's the third time this month. Dammit, that water hole is on our land, and it's for our cattle, not a bunch of wild mustangs."

His companion reached for his arm as he pulled the rifle from the back seat. "Bill, what're you doing?"

"I'm done with this crap, Mona, and I'm tired of mending this damn fence. I'm gonna put a stop to it right now."

"How do you expect to find that herd on foot?"

"There's a piece of that wire missing, and there's blood on the ground. I'd say one of them got hooked up in the wire. With any luck at all it'll be that friggin' stallion. Bring them field glasses and come on." Unhappy about it, she pulled out the binoculars and hurried after him.

NOT TOO FAR AWAY, SOMEBODY else had already found the horses. The lead stallion was down, tangled in the barbed wire, the rest of the herd had moved off a way, enjoying the warm sun and the lush grass. "Derek, you be careful, that stallion could take you apart in a heartbeat."

"I know, Jill, but he's caught up in that wire, hobbled himself, and he's bleeding. We've got to get him loose."

4

"Derek, no. Look, we need the others. You stay here, and I'll go for help. Please don't do anything foolish. Wait here, keep an eye on him until I get back with the others."

"All right, but make it quick." Without another word, she wheeled her horse and rode away, the wild horses parting to give her plenty of room.

As soon as she disappeared from sight, he dismounted and began to slowly approach the stallion, cooing softly to the injured animal. "Easy now, Big Red, easy now. You're all tangled up there. I'll bet that hurts. Easy now, just be still and I'll get that wire off you."

Up on the ridge someone else had found the man and the horses. He settled down and began to take careful aim. "Bill, for Christ's sake, what the hell are you doing?"

"Hush now, Mona. I'm gonna kill two birds with one stone."

"You're going to shoot him? Jesus, Bill ..."

"No, I'm not going to shoot him, for god's sake. See that big green rock beside the stallion? I'm gonna hit that. The damn horse will kick the shit out of that fool and try to run away. That'll give me a clear shot at it. That jackass'll get beat up, the stallion will be coyote meat, and no one'll ever know for sure what happened."

"Bill, don't do this, this's plain crazy."

"Just shut the hell up and watch through them field glasses. Tell me when he gets close enough to the horse."

Down on the grassland, Derek Wheeler was moving closer to the trapped animal. "Easy now, Big Red, easy." His pulse was racing, for he knew how dangerous a wild mustang could be if cornered and frightened. "Easy now." This horse was caught and definitely frightened, its eyes rolled back in terror.

He eased closer and extended his hand toward the horse's injured leg. The stallion screamed and lunged at him just as a shot rang out and the small boulder beside them exploded.

"Jesus Christ, Bill, what happened?"

"I don't know. Never seen anything like that before."

She was dragging at his arm. "Come on, we have to get the hell out of here. That man's surely dead; nobody could survive that. Hurry, we've got to get gone before somebody sees us and reports it to the police. We'll be charged with murder. Come on."

It sank into his shocked brain that she was right, and he hurried after her. Throwing the rifle in the back seat, he leaped behind the wheel and drove swiftly away.

An hour later the young woman returned with several more riders, but the stallion was gone and so was her boyfriend. There was nothing but a fine layer of green dust where the horse had lain. His horse was quietly grazing with the wild herd.

Jillian Arbend called and called, she tried his phone and heard it ringing. It was on the ground with the rest of his clothes, covered in the green dust. "What the hell?" She dismounted and picked up the shirt and jeans, shaking the dust off them.

"What is it, Jill?"

"Derek's clothes, his phone, even his boots are here, but there's no sign of him or the stallion. I don't get it. Even if he managed to free the horse, why would he strip off to ride it, as if that horse would let him. Where did he go? Why naked, and where the hell is the horse?"

"That looks like him coming there," said one of the other riders.

Jillian looked up to see the stallion on the top of the ridge, silhouetted against the setting sun. The horse bugled a call and the herd turned as one to go to him. As the herd of mustangs crossed over the ridge, the red stallion trotted down to where the riders sat atop their horses.

Slowly, cautiously, he approached Jillian. She reached out her hand and, tentatively, he approached, stretching out his neck so he could sniff at her. For just a moment he put his soft muzzle into her palm then snorted and raced away to join the herd. Almost in shock, she stood and watched as he disappeared over the ridge.

"Jill, what the hell just happened? Nobody's been able to get within a hundred yards of that horse before. He almost acted as though he knew you."

"I don't know, Merle. I really don't. What I do know is I have to find Derek. Let's spread out and start looking."

"He ain't here, Jill," said another rider. "Sun's going down, we'll find nothing today. We need to go back, report this to the sheriff, and get back here at first light with a real search party."

"Peggy's right, Jill," said Merle. "Let's get back now and set up for a proper search in the morning." Peggy and Merle were like family. Jillian sighed and allowed them to lead her away.

THE SHERIFF JUST SHOOK his head as he listened to the people explain about the disappearance of Derek Wheeler. Had it just been one of them he might have laughed it off as them smoking too much weed, but he knew several of these folks. None of it made any sense, but he believed them.

"All right, Merle, I'll make some calls, set up a search party for tomorrow. First, though, I want to have a hard look at the place where you say you found his clothes. If this is some kind of joke, or prank, I warn you, I have no sense of humor at all."

"It's not a joke, Sheriff," declared Jill. "The horse was down, tangled up in a length of barbed wire. We agreed that Derek would keep watch while I went for help. I know him too well. He's tried to set that horse free all by himself, and something went horribly wrong."

"Like what?"

"Sheriff, I have no idea at all. None. All I know is, he's gone, his clothes were left behind, scattered around like he'd been torn out of them, and there's no sign of him anywhere."

"Was there blood at the scene?"

"Only what had been there when we first found the horse."

"And the area was covered with greenish powder?"

"That's right."

"Anything else unusual?"

"No, I don't think ... wait, there was a small boulder right by the horse. It was a greenish color, but it wasn't there when we got back."

"Greenish? Like the powder?"

"Yeah, like the rock exploded into dust. Weird. Sheriff, can't we start looking for him tonight?"

"Miss, I'm sorry, but I can't even call him a missing person for forty-eight hours, besides, I don't want that crime scene getting all trampled up."

"Crime scene?"

"Yes, ma'am, by calling it a crime scene I can legally begin a search tomorrow. I follow the rules, check it out, then we start the search. It's that or wait out the forty-eight hours."

Jill gazed at him incredulously with huge eyes. "All right, Sheriff, crime scene it is." She turned and walked out of his office.

"Jill, wait," called Peggy, as she followed her out the door.

The emotion and frustration suddenly boiled over and Jillian fairly fell into Peggy's arms. "Oh, Peg, what am I going to do? Derek could be hurt, lost, ..."

"Easy, honey, easy. We'll find him. First thing we can see daylight, we'll be on horseback, looking for him. If he's out there, we'll find him. Honey, you go home and get some sleep, you're exhausted. We'll pick you up first thing in the morning." Jillian sniffed, kissed Peggy's cheek, then stepped back and turned away to Derek's old truck. Somehow she managed to fend off the tears until she got back home.

WHILE JILL RETURNED to pace about her apartment, the stallion stood beneath a tree, head down, but not sleeping. "I'm a horse, I'm really a fucking horse. How the hell did this happen? What am I going to do? How the hell do I change back? Can I ever change back? Oh god ... Jill. She must be worried sick by now. She'll try to find me; I know she will. If I go hang out where I was, she'll come back.

"How do I tell her what happened? How can I make her understand? How ..." The yowl of a hungry puma interrupted that line of thought. He gave a snort and began to urge the herd out into the open grassland again. It would be easier to escape from there, and harder for the cat to find cover.

With the herd out in the moonlight, the horse turned to face the trees. The cat stood glaring back, but it was old and toothless, and no match for the stallion facing it. It turned back to look for smaller prey.

Dawn found him lying comfortably in the tall grass, watching the sunrise. He stood, shook himself, gave a soft call then trotted away, the herd following his lead. He was headed for water.

Once again there was a fence blocking his path, but the mind driving the stallion was different now. He couldn't sense any danger near, so he closely inspected the fence and posts. The search showed what he needed, a slightly rotting post. He turned his back, took careful aim then lashed out. With a loud crack the post snapped off and dangled loosely, held partially up by the wire.

A moment later another post was down, and so was the fence. The herd carefully picked their hooves up as they stepped across the former barrier then trotted off to the waterhole. The stallion stood watching while the herd drank their fill then, he too, approached the water's edge. One last look around for danger, then he too lowered his head to the sweet water.

Once he'd had his fill, the stallion took his herd into the hills, away from prying eyes. He needed to think, try to understand what had happened. They were grazing quietly when a shot rang out. There was a yelp nearby and a wounded coyote dragged itself into view. A second shot finished the coyote, but the horses were already in full flight.

The stallion raced along; the herd strung out behind him. He rounded a boulder and a small boy stood directly in his path. A woman screamed, and the boy froze in terror. Big Red skidded to a stop just inches from the boy. The herd split apart and thundered past them, leaving the boy unharmed.

Reaching out, the horse gently rubbed the boy's cheek with a soft nose, then bolted away, leaving the woman to gather the boy into her arms and wonder at what had just happened.

"Damn, that was too close," thought Derek as he raced along. *"What kind of a moron takes his family when he goes out shooting coyotes? He's not supposed to be doing that anyway. I should go back and kick his sorry ass."*

Even as he had that thought, the stallion's instincts took over and carried him further away from the man with the gun. Later, as the sun was down, he led the herd back towards the water.

Mystery

The herd spent the night near where he'd been changed. Dawn came, and with it the search party. The stallion raised his head at the sound of off-road vehicles. He turned and raced toward the herd, urging them to action. As the ATVs approached the place where he'd disappeared, Derek Wheeler gave in to the stallion's natural caution and urged the herd away.

The horses disappeared over the ridge as the people stopped and began to investigate the area. He turned and looked back. "Jill." She was there, Jill was there with them, and it pulled at him, the need to see her, to tell her what had happened to him, to ask her for help.

Jillian stood aside, fuming while the sheriff and his deputies poked around, took pictures, and checked out Derek's clothing which was still there. They'd also brought tracking dogs. A sigh of frustration escaped her lips as she wandered away to let them work. That's when she noticed the big red stallion trotting toward her.

The others gazed in wonder as the magnificent horse approached Jill. She stood very still, her hand outstretched, as he tentatively drew nearer. Cautiously, he stretched out to put a soft muzzle into the palm of her hand. Cooing soothing sounds, she took a step closer and ran her hand over his cheek. Just then one of the dogs barked and the stallion exploded away at a gallop.

"Shit," she muttered, as she kicked at a clump of grass.

11

"I can't understand it," said a voice at her shoulder. "That horse has been as elusive as a ghost for the past five years, but he sure seems to have taken a shine to you, Jill."

"I don't know, Merle, I don't understand it either, but I have the strangest feeling about this. Like you said before, the first few times I saw that horse, I couldn't get within a mile of him. Since Derek disappeared, it's like he's trying to tell me something. I think that horse was still here when whatever happened, happened, and I think he's trying to tell me."

"So you're the horse whisperer now, or is he the human whisperer?"

"Shut up, Merle." She walked a few steps in the direction of the ridge where the horse had disappeared. "What are you trying to tell me, Big Red? You know what happened to Derek, don't you?"

Derek was unhappy with the horse's instinctive flight. Jill was there and he'd felt her touch. The stallion didn't care how he felt about it. Humans meant danger; he'd tolerated all he could then he'd fled to the safety of the open plains.

THE SEARCH PARTIES went over the area carefully, they used dogs, drones, and a hunter/tracker of high reputation, but there was no sign of Derek Wheeler. During that time the red stallion, in spite of Derek's misgivings, led his herd far away from all the human activity.

"So that's it? You're just giving up?"

The sheriff sighed deeply. "Miss, I'm sorry. I am, but there's nothing else I can do. We've gone over that area a dozen times in the past week and there's no sign of him. I've put out an APB to every police force in the country. They'll all be watching for him, but I just don't see what else you expect me to do."

"Nothing," she said, as she turned on her heel and strode to the door. "Not a fucking thing." She slammed the door behind her, then got in Derek's aging truck and burned out. A short time later she was putting a heavy backpack into the bed of the truck.

One of Derek's friends saw her loading up. "Jill, what the hell are you doing?"

"Going camping," was the terse reply.

"Girl, that's such a bad idea."

"To hell with you, Harvey, all of you. Derek's your friend, and he's in trouble. All you guys want to do is sit around swilling beer and reminisce about what a great guy he was, and what a terrible loss to the group. Fuck you, fuck you all. I'm going to find Derek."

He reached out to grip her arm and stop her. "Girl, that's just foolish. It's no place for a woman alone and on foot, out in those hills."

"Get your hands off me, Harvey or I'll kick you so hard you'll be wearing your balls for a bowtie. I'm going to find Derek and neither you nor anybody else is going to stop me."

"Hell, girl," he sighed, as he released her arm and backed away, "you don't even know where to look. The whole posse went over that area with a fine-toothed comb. He ain't there."

"Maybe not, but Big Red knows where he is."

"The horse? The horse knows where he is, and he'll tell you? For god's sake woman, give your head a shake."

"That's right, that stallion knows what happened to Derek, and I know he'll take me to him."

"Jill, nobody's seen that herd for days. All that search party activity has driven them to higher ground. God only knows where that horse is now."

"Then I'll ask God to show me where to find him." With that, she started the truck and drove away.

Jill returned to where Derek had disappeared. Any evidence had long since vanished, taken by the sheriff, or trampled into oblivion by the search parties. It didn't matter, she wasn't looking for evidence, she was looking for horses.

The last time Jill had seen Big Red, he'd disappeared over that ridge. She settled the huge backpack on her shoulders then set out. At the top of the ridge all she saw was more grassland and hills. Those horses could be anywhere.

The pack thumped on the ground as she dropped it. Jill pulled out her topographical map and studied the area, nothing stood out, so she sighed and put it away. Ah well, they'd need water, and she thought she could see a creek in the distance through the binoculars. She shouldered the pack and set out, at least it was mostly downhill.

That night Jill made a lonely camp and cried herself to sleep. "Derek, I know you're out there somewhere, and I will find you. I swear to god I will."

While Jill set out on her search, Derek had little else to do except think, ponder his fate. At length he concluded the horse had acted rightly. If the humans discovered what he was they'd haul him off to some secret lab and he'd never see the light of day again. Derek Wheeler set himself to mourn the loss of his lover, and the life he'd always known. He steeled himself for a life on the run, keeping out of sight, staying hidden from humans.

FOR JILL, IT WAS EASIER said than done, but on the sixth day, as her food was running low, she spotted the herd of horses. For the rest of the day, she followed them, slowly getting closer.

The stallion was aware of her and watchful, but he didn't come near. Derek fought his natural urge to run to her, he had to stay away, for her sake as well as her own.

As darkness fell and the herd settled down, Jill slowly approached. She got quite close before he lost that internal battle and blocked her path.

"Hey there, Big Red. Easy boy. It's me, Jill. You know me, we're friends, right? Easy now." She stood still as he cautiously approached and sniffed at her, then to her great surprise, he nuzzled at her and laid down.

Jill stroked the magnificent animal's neck and back, then settled to the ground beside him. "You know, don't you, sweetheart. You big, beautiful beast, you know what happened to my Derek, don't you? That's what you've been trying to tell me. Where is he, Red? Is he hurt? Can you show me where he is?"

The only answer she got was a soft whicker, and a nose rubbed gently along her arm. "All right, Big Red, it's dark now. We'll take this up again in the morning. Just don't roll over in your sleep and squish me." She carefully unrolled her sleeping bag and crawled in. When she awakened at dawn, Derek was lying beside her, naked, and shivering.

"Derek! Oh my god, Derek." Jill wrapped her arms around the weeping man and hugged him tightly. "You're freezing. God, get in here with me and get warm."

She tried to pull him into the sleeping bag with her, but he took her gently by the shoulders to stop her. "Jill, Jill honey, listen to me. Listen. I can't hold this form for long. Please listen. Jill, you have to go away and forget me."

"What? I'll never forget you, Derek. I love you. I searched for you for days and days, and I ..."

"Jill. Listen to me, just listen. I can't hold this for long. Jill, I don't know how it happened, but I'm blended with the stallion, more him that me most of the time."

"What? What do you mean you're blended with the horse? Derek, we need to go back. We can get help ..."

"Jill, no. Lover, listen to me. If I go back they'll put me in a lab somewhere and experiment on me. I'll never see the light of day again. At least out here, I'm free. Jill, I need time, time to understand what's happened, time to ... shit, I'm losing it. Get back."

A moment later he shimmered into the stallion once again. The horse stood gazing sadly at her as she began to nibble on the last protein bar and gather her things.

Tears ran down her face as Jill packed up her camping gear. She was out of food, she had to go back, but now that she'd found Derek, she had to find a way to help him. Jill stood and swung the pack onto her back.

"I need to go get more supplies, but I'll come right back. Derek, I'm not going to abandon you. I'll come back, and we'll figure this out together." She turned and started away.

Jill stopped and turned around at the snort so close behind her. The stallion was kneeling, gazing at her, as though telling her to mount up. Hesitantly, she stepped toward him and leaned against him. He reached back and pushed her butt into the air with his nose.

That made her laugh. "All right, Big Red, but you be gentle with me." She swung her leg across his back and he surged to his feet. With Jill clinging to his mane and back, he set out at a canter. At his bugling call, the herd followed.

All through the day he ran, the herd pacing behind, uncomplaining. The hills rolled by and the sun crossed the sky, but still the mighty stallion didn't tire, nor did he stop for food or water.

Jill's bones ached from the constant bouncing of the pack on her back, but she made no complaint. As the sun began to slide below the hills, Jill saw the old truck in the distance. The big horse slowed to a walk as he approached.

She slid to the ground, catching hold of his mane again to steady herself for a moment. With a thump, the backpack landed in the truck bed. Jill turned and hugged the horse's neck. "I'll come back, lover. I swear I will. I just need a week to do some research, but I'll come back. Promise me you'll stay in this general area."

He tossed his head and snorted then turned away to his herd. They were heading toward the water hole. Noticing the fence keeping the horses away from the water, Jill put the bumper of the truck against a post and pushed it over. As she drove away she saw him lead the herd across the downed fence toward the dammed-up stream.

Research

"Jill, you're back. We were just about to send out the search parties. Where the hell have you been?" She climbed slowly from the old truck to be met with a barrage of questions from her friends.

"You know where I went, Merle," she sighed, as she heaved the backpack from the truck bed and tried to get it onto her shoulders. She failed, and it slipped to the ground.

"You're beat to a pulp, girl," said Peggy. "Let me get that for you." She swept up the pack and slung it over her own shoulder. "Merle, get the door open for her. We'll put some food into her then let her sleep for a week."

With a nod, Merle Decker took the keys from Jillian's hand and unlocked the door to her building. They followed her inside, then unlocked her apartment door. Peggy guided Jillian to a comfortable chair and she gratefully sank into it. "You stay right there and rest while I fix you something to eat. Merle."

"Yes, dear?"

"Don't use that tone with me, mister," she grinned. "You go gas up that truck then put it in the parking lot for her. Go on now."

"Yes, dear," he said, and winked at Jillian as he stepped out the door.

"Men," grinned Peggy, "can't live with 'em, can't shoot 'em. Speaking of men, I see you came home alone. No sign of Derek, I take it. How about the horses? You find Big Red?" She brought Jillian a plate of hot food and a tall glass of milk. "Here, get this inside you and you'll feel a lot better."

18

Jill tucked in like a woman starved. "Mmm, god that's good. Thanks Peg. Yeah, took me a few days, but I found the herd."

"Red still your best friend?"

"Yep. I can walk right up to him. That horse is trying to tell me something, but I just can't understand him. I need to get a few days of sleep then hit the books and internet."

"Going to learn to speak horse?"

"With any luck at all. Peggy, Derek's out there. They didn't find a body, so he's out there somewhere, and I plan to figure this out."

"Maybe some horse rustlers got him. There's a bunch operating in the area, rounding up wild broncs and selling them for dog food. Maybe some of them took him."

"And left all his clothes?"

"Girl rustlers?"

Jillian laughed at that. "Shut up, Peg. Shut up or I'll make you come with me next time."

"You're going out there again?"

"I've got some serious research to do first, but yeah, I'll be going out again."

"Jill, honey, we won't try to stop you, but next time come to the ranch first, take one of our horses. You can cover a lot more ground on horseback than on foot. Promise me now."

"All right, Mamma Peg, next time I'll take a horse."

Merle returned and dropped her keys on the kitchen counter. "Let's go, Merle. Girl needs a couple days rest, then we'll give her the third degree." Peggy linked her arm through his and led him out. The door clicked softly behind them.

Jill rose heavily from the chair, deposited the empty plate and glass in the sink, then made her way to the bedroom and stripped off. The shower was heavenly, and she stood there until the hot water was gone. She toweled off then returned to the bedroom and crawled under the covers. It was past noon the next day when she awakened. By three o'clock she was deep into her research.

For several days, Jill rarely left her computer, unless it was to go to the library in search of rare or obscure books. She read everything she could find on shapeshifters, were-animals, then shifted into a study of horse psychology. Two days of that gave her a better understanding of what might be driving Derek. She then returned to shapeshifters. By then, she'd triggered an alarm.

SEVERAL PEOPLE WERE in the Great Hall. The vampire king sat back, enjoying his coffee and the voices of the people gathered there. "All right, Clara, you and the Lady Hawk are far too pleased with yourselves. What have you done now?"

The small woman smiled brightly and adjusted her glasses. "Well, Sire, we've developed a theory about how the werewolves came to be."

"Are you planning to share with the rest of us?" asked the queen.

"Yes, ma'am. You see, the werewolves aren't immortal like the vampires or the shapeshifters like Ronni and Torvil. We know that Ella, the original vampire, as well as Ronni and Torvil, all came to the change through the exploding meteorite. The result is a shapeshifter who is immortal, and yet barren, unable to reproduce.

"The werewolves, however, are long lived, but they're mortal, and they do reproduce in the regular way. These are the facts as we know them.

"Now, here's what we believe happened. Somewhere back in the past, a pregnant woman was changed into were-wolf. We believe that the fetus, female, could have survived the change. She was born with the ability to shapeshift, and was able to pass that along to her offspring.

"As we know, the wolf strain is dominant, but humans and werewolves are quite compatible reproductively. We believe it's through that child that the wolves were able to come into being."

"Interesting, and highly plausible," mused the king, "but it presents a problem."

"Oh?"

"What of the original mother? She would be immortal, would she not?"

"Yes, Sire, I believe that's true."

"Then out there, somewhere, we have another shapeshifter, an immortal werewolf."

Clara polished her glasses then resettled them on her face. "Yes, I do believe that's true. I ..." She got no further as a nearby computer beeped loudly.

Tommy Dawson, known in the vampire king's castle as the court sorcerer, reacted instantly to the *beep* from his computer. His fingers flew and screen after screen appeared and disappeared with speed as he searched. A moment later he stopped on a page of code.

Igor, the alpha of the werewolf pack that served the king, was looking over Tommy's shoulder. "That can't be good."

"Indeed not, my sorcerer's apprentice," sighed Tommy. "Indeed, it cannot."

"Gentlemen, talk to me," came the deep voice of the king, as he leaned forward in his chair to rest his elbows on the table.

"Sorry, Sire," said Tommy, as he turned to face the powerfully built man. "We've got somebody researching shapeshifters. She's thorough, and determined, as well as a skilled researcher. She's been focusing on the werewolves, but not exclusively. She seems to have an interest in horses as well, but her main focus is on the possibility of shapeshifting."

The queen suddenly grabbed the king's arm and nodded. He gave her a slight nod to show he understood. "Damn the technology, anyway. Can you find out who and where she is?"

"Oh yes, my King, I can. Just a moment and I'll ..."

"Got her," said Igor, grinning as he turned from the screen. "Her name is Jillian Arbend, and she's in a town called Riverton, Utah." As Igor announced the woman's name there was a crash. The girl carrying a tray of refreshments dropped it and covered her mouth with her hand.

All eyes turned to the woman who blushed deeply and began to clean up the mess. The queen came to help her, as did several others. Queen Sally gathered the distraught woman in her arms while the others cleaned up what had been dropped. "Elaine, hush now, it's all right."

"My queen, I'm so sorry. Please, let me clean this up and go for more. I didn't ..."

"Hush now, Sally's got you. It's all right, we can deal with that later. Come now, come sit by me and tell the king what startled you so when you heard that woman's name. You know her, don't you?"

"Yes, ma'am, I do," she replied as she sat and composed herself. "She's my sister."

"She's at it again," said Tommy. "What do you want me to do, Sire?"

"Shut her down, Tommy. Elaine, call your sister and see if you can find out what she's up to. I promise you, we won't hurt her, but we do need to know what's going on, and we need to divert her attention."

"Of course, Sire." Elaine pulled her phone from her pocket and turned it on. A moment later she had it on speaker and was waiting for her sister to answer.

"Hello, Elaine?"

"Yes, Jill, it's me."

"Elaine, this isn't a good time for ... noooooo, god fucking dammit to hell." They could hear her as she started crying, repeating the word *no* over and over. Tommy turned away from his screen and nodded to the king.

Elaine tried to break through her sister's despair. "Jill, Jill listen. Jillian Arbend, you stop that right now and listen to me."

"You don't understand. My computer just fried, I've lost all my research, and ..."

"I do understand, and that research is why your computer fried. Stop this and listen to me."

"What do you mean, my research is why my computer fried. What the hell is ..."

"Jillian, for the love of god, will you shut up and listen to me."

There was a soft sniff then a contrite voice. "I'm listening."

"Are you at home?"

"What? Yes, I'm at the apartment."

"Do you have somewhere to go, somewhere safe?"

"What, Elaine, what ...?"

"Jill, listen. I'm with my employer right now."

"So?"

"Jill, your research triggered an alarm here, and it's these people who shut down your computer."

"What? Why the hell would they burn me? What would make them burn me? I don't understand."

"Jillian," said a deep commanding voice. "My name is Harald Eldredsson. My people destroyed your computer for a number of reasons. First to prevent further research, and second to protect you from other prying eyes than ours."

"But ..."

"Let me explain. You've been researching shapeshifters. The intensity of your search, and the power of your reaction to losing the research, tells me you've recently been in contact with a shapeshifter, probably someone close to you, am I correct?"

"You'd believe me?" Her voice was soft, and so hopeful, and yet frightened.

"I do, and I can also offer you some help. Do you have a safe place to go where no one will find you?"

"Well, I guess I could try, but why?"

"Others may also have discovered your research and will want to know why. I offer you protection and assistance, your sister is not only an employee, but a valued friend as well. Will you trust her faith in me?"

"I ... Elaine?"

"Honey, please, you need help, I can hear that in your voice. These people can help you, and I'd trust any one of them with my life. Please let us help you."

The woman sighed then gave a soft, "Okay."

"Jill, what happened?"

"I have no idea. It's Derek. He disappeared."

"Oh god, no."

"All we found of him were his clothes, and the horse was gone too, so I tracked it down, and it turned into Derek, but he couldn't hold his human form ..." She stopped speaking and started crying again.

"Oh my god," gasped Elaine. "Derek's her boyfriend. They've been together for years. Oh Jill."

The king stepped in again. "Jillian, I'll send people to you. They'll help you to understand what's happened, and they'll help you get your lover back. Elaine will be with them. Is there an airport near?"

"Yes."

"Leave your home and go to the safe place. As soon as they're on the ground, Elaine will call to arrange a place to meet. Be at peace, girl, help is on the way."

"Okay. Thank you."

Elaine sighed as she returned her phone to her pocket. "Sire, thank you for helping my sister. She and Derek are inseparable."

"Go pack a bag, Elaine, I'll set things in motion."

"Sire, I can't thank you enough."

"Go," he smiled as he patted her hand. "All right, Terry, Gudrun, and her team are in New York, and Mother is with them. Looks like you're up, Igor. Choose your team."

The young agent smiled. "I'll need the Lady Hawk, Larise and Bran as well, Amanda, and Miss Marlene."

"Me?" asked the small redhead who was lounging in her chair.

"Da, you're the only available vampire at the moment, and we'll need somebody who can use the compulsion. I'll do my best to ..."

"Don't say it, Igor," she replied, seeing the teasing twinkle in his eye, "and don't even think it in Russian. Sure, I'll go, why not? Lilly's buried in a new book, and it'll be a couple of weeks before she finishes the first draft. I'm in."

"All right. Sire, what are the objectives?"

"First, make certain the government or the media hasn't clued in on this."

"I can work some of that from here, Sire," said Tommy.

"Excellent. Second; Igor, find that were-horse, bring him and the woman here if you can."

"And if I can't?"

"Do what's needed, but bring the woman, unharmed for Elaine's sake."

"Da, I understand, King Harald. We'll find a way to bring them both. Get moving, people. We're on the clock with this one."

As Igor hurried from the hall the queen reached for and squeezed the king's hand. A knowing glance passed between them.

WHILE JILLIAN WAS DOING her research, the stallion kept his small herd close to the area where she'd left them. Unfortunately, her knocking down the fence brought unwanted attention to the horses.

Bill and Mona Higgins stood looking at the broken posts and tangled wire. Bill was swearing and occasionally kicking at the broken post.

Mona broke into his frustrated tirade. "That post was pushed over from the road. It wasn't the horses who did this. What'd you think, rustlers looking for dog food money?"

Bill sighed and gave another half-hearted kick. "Yeah, I guess, maybe. That's not a bad idea though."

"Bill?"

"Look, I know a guy. Those horses are staying close, using our water, and busting down our fences. I'll help those guys take down the herd. We'll get a few dollars to make fence repairs and we'll be rid of the horses. There'll be no further need to worry after that."

"Dammit, Bill. If you get caught you could go to jail. We could lose the ranch. Just take down the fence and let the horses use the watering hole. They can't drink it all."

"That's not the point, Mona. It's the principal of the thing. This is my land, and I own the water rights to it. That's my watering hole, I built it for my cattle. Damn wild horses anyway, using up grassland and water I could use to run more cattle on. No, girl, I'm gittin' rid of those damn mustangs once and for all."

Three nights later, a truck slowly crawled past the broken fence then stopped. Men got out and opened the back, lowering a ramp and setting up guide fences they pulled from the truck that followed them. In the dim light the stallion stood watching. He soon began to quietly get the herd moving away. Once he had them pointed in the right direction he bugled a call and sped away, the herd racing along behind him.

Back at the truck, Bill Higgins was swearing again. "Something must have spooked them," growled a voice.

"Spooked, nothin'," muttered Bill. "It was that damn stallion; he must've seen us settin' up."

"Yeah, well, we ain't done yet. Arlo, get that friggin' drone in the air. Arlo'll fly that thing out in front of the herd and turn them. Afore you know it, they'll come running right into the truck."

A moment later the drone was in the air, pursuing the horses. It wasn't long before the stallion saw it coming at them from the side. Some of the herd started to turn away, but the big horse ignored it and kept going. He knew what it was and what it was trying to do.

The drone managed to scatter the herd a couple of times, but each time the stallion called, and they returned to him as he continued to put more distance between them and the truck. Finally, in frustration, the man at the controls sent the drone right at the stallion's head.

As the machine bore down on him the horse tensed, suddenly spun around, leaped into the air, and lashed out with both back legs. The drone exploded on impact. Back at the truck the men heard the bugled challenge of the big red horse as he reared up and brought both front hooves down on the damaged drone.

He then led his herd into the hills. He could no longer wait for Jill; she'd have to find him on her own.

Contact with a Different World

Jillian Arbend sat staring at her phone for a long moment then rose from her chair, swept up her purse and keys, then left the building. She headed straight for Merle and Peggy's old horse ranch. When she arrived, she pulled the truck around to the back of the house out of sight.

Peg stepped out to greet her. "Howdy stranger, long time no see."

Jill climbed out of the truck, looked over her shoulder, then walked toward the house. "Yeah, it's been a few days since I came up for air. Can we go inside?"

"Sure, honey, come on in. Like a beer?"

"I would, thanks."

"Jesus, Jill, you look like something scared the shit out of you," said Merle, as he opened a beer and passed it to her.

"Thanks. Yup, that's pretty much what happened."

"So, tell us about it," said Peggy, but Jillian just sighed and wouldn't make eye-contact. "Look, Jill, we're here for you, you know that. Hell, me and Merle practically raised you and Elaine. You know us. If you can't trust us, then who can you to turn to?"

Jill studied her beer bottle for a few moments then spoke. "All right, but you guys have to promise to listen. You have to suspend all judgment and belief, and listen, okay? You're not allowed to call the cops, the military, or the guys with the butterfly nets and straight jackets."

28

They were both paying close attention now. Peggy nodded, so Jill went on. "I did find Derek out there."

"What? Is he okay? Why didn't you bring him back with you?"

"Shut up, Merle. Just shut up and listen. Yes, I found him, but I found the horses first. Big Red was friendly, and when I lay down for the night, he laid down close by. When I woke up next morning, Derek was laying where the horse had been, buck naked.

"I went all gushy over him and we both cried, but he wouldn't come back with me. He said he couldn't hold his human form for long."

"What?"

"Hush, Merle, let her talk. Go on, Jill."

"Well, I was staring at him, wondering what the hell he was talking about when he just started to shimmer, and then he was Big Red again. He knelt down so I could climb on his back, then he carried me back to the truck."

"Ah-huh."

"Merle, just shut up and listen or I'll shoot you in the ass, first chance I get. There's more.

"When I got back, you guys were there, fed me, then I slept until noon the next day. After that I started researching shapeshifters on the internet. I was at it for days, and I had a massive amount of material to study when my phone rang. That was this morning.

"It was Elaine on the phone, but just as I answered it, my computer fried. I lost everything. I was bawling like a baby, and Elaine was trying to get me to listen, when a man came on the phone, the guy she works for.

"Now, here's the real crazy part. He said he knew what happened, that it was his people who fried my computer. He said it was obvious I'd seen a shapeshifter, and they'd fried my computer to protect me from anybody else cluing in to what I was doing.

"He said he'd send people to help me, help me understand what had happened, and help me to get Derek back, help him learn control of the change. He said Elaine would be with them, and that she'd call as soon as they landed. He wanted me to stay out of sight until they get here."

"Jesus, for real?"

"For real, Merle. Look, I know Elaine's trusted the wrong kind before, but I get the sense she's clear on these people."

"So, why'd you come to us and not just hide out, keep the secret?"

"Because, Merle old buddy, Elaine might trust those people, but I trust you guys, and I have a favor to ask, a big one."

"Sure, sweetie, whatever you need," said Peggy, "you know that. What's up?"

"I want to bring Derek here, to the ranch."

"Here?"

"This is a horse ranch, another horse in the barn won't raise any eyebrows, and I'll be able to stay with him until he can master the change. I'll ..." She got no further as her phone buzzed. "Elaine?"

"It's me, Jill. Are you safe?"

"Yeah, I'm good. How the hell did you get here so fast?"

"In a private plane, experimental, super sonic, scary fast. Where are you?"

"I'm at the ranch. Look, I've told Peg and Merle everything. We should meet here."

"Half an hour. I love you, little sister. You be careful."

"You too," replied Jill, but the connection was already broken.

"THEY'RE AT THE RANCH. Peggy and Merle practically raised us after Mom died and Dad hit the bottle. She'll be safe there. Igor, she told them everything."

"Great, can nobody keep a secret anymore?"

"She trusts them, Igor. I've made a few bad choices in who I chose to trust before. She'll be with them, and they'll be watching to see who's coming. What do you want to do?"

"Do you trust these people, Elaine?"

"Yes, utterly."

"Then we go. When we get there, you can go in first to put them at ease. If that fails, then Miss Marlene will have to convince them to trust us."

Marlene grinned and winked at Elaine. "Please don't hurt them, Marlene, they're good people."

"I'll be good, I promise." Seeing the look of concern on Elaine's face, Marlene relented. "I will, Elaine. I won't hurt them; I swear it to you."

Elaine nodded and thanked her as Rhonda returned with two sets of car keys. Amanda drove one car and Elaine the other. When they reached the ranch driveway, Elaine pulled over and called Jillian.

"Jill, honey, the two cars at the driveway are our people. We're coming in now, okay?"

"Okay."

Elaine dropped her phone back in her pocket and turned to Igor. "How do you want to do this?"

"Your sister has told too many people. This is disturbing. You go in first with Miss Amanda and Miss Marlene. Miss Marlene, perhaps you could suggest these folks keep our secrets safe, yeah?"

"Got it, Boss," she grinned, as she winked at Rhonda.

"My pretty bird, would you go up for a look around and make sure there are no unwanted observers in the area?"

"On it, my lover." Rhonda kissed his cheek then leaped skyward. Igor nodded then Elaine took Marlene and Amanda with her up the long driveway. They pulled around the house and parked beside Jillian's old truck.

Jill opened the door and motioned them in. She hugged Elaine fiercely. "Oh gods, it is you, it really is you. I haven't seen you in three years."

Elaine smiled warmly as she returned the hug. "I know, sweetie, I know. Put me down now, and I'll introduce you. Folks, this is Amanda, and this is Marlene. Please listen up for a minute, Marlene has something to tell you."

They looked at Marlene then froze in fear. She spoke in a demonic voice that demanded instant obedience. *"Peggy, Merle, and Jillian, pay attention. You have been told much, and you will learn more in the coming days. You will hold all you learn about us secret. You will never speak aloud or write down any of what you will learn. Do you understand?"*

"We understand. Keep you and everything about you secret."

"You will now relax with us, know that we are here to help."

"Wow, what the hell was that?"

"That, Merle, was what we call the compulsion. I'm sorry to have to do that, but for the moment we can't take any chances."

"Fair enough, so what about the rest of your people."

"I'll call them in," smiled Elaine. "Igor didn't want to scare you with all of us showing up at once."

She pulled out her phone and called.

"Igor."

"All clear, Boss, come on in."

The second car pulled up behind the house and the rest of the team entered. Igor held the door open and a hawk sailed in, then transformed into a naked woman. "Now that's an entrance," grinned Marlene. "So, delicious, are you going to stay naked, or do you want your clothes?"

Wide-eyed, Rhonda looked down at her body. "Oh crap, be right back, folks." She hurried out the door and soon returned in a long sun dress and sandals. "Sorry about that. You sort of get used to the nudity when you're a shapeshifter."

"Ah-huh," grunted Merle.

Peggy slapped him on the arm. "Put your eyes back in your head, old man. So, young miss, I guess that was your way of convincing us that shapeshifters are real."

"Did it work?"

"Oh, it worked all right. I think my poor husband went blind, but it worked." Merle blushed and the others had a good chuckle at his expense. "So, are all you folks shapeshifters?"

"No, not all of us," said Amanda. "Elaine, Larise, and I are human."

"That's good to know," said Merle. "What about you guys?" He was addressing Igor.

"Both Bran and I are werewolves."

"And you, young miss? What else can you do besides that voice thing?"

"You don't want to know, Merle," she replied, as she patted his hand.

"All right, so the pleasantries are over, now to the business at hand," said Igor. "Jillian, your research triggered alarms at out headquarters. We had to shut you down before anyone else got interested."

"Who are we talking about here, Agent Wolf?"

"The government for one, crime syndicates for another. The government would want to study the shifter, learn how to create others, how to train them as weapons, spies, and more. The criminals would want to control the shifter, to use them for gain and profit."

"So, what makes you the good guys?"

"We're shifters ourselves, among other things. The man you spoke to is our king, king of all the non-human folk. It's his belief that non-humans need to remain as legend only, not to be found out by the general population.

"We keep ourselves secret from the government and the criminals for good reason. As a child I, and many others were captured by criminals, tortured, and trained as assassins. You can see why we want to remain hidden.

"On the other hand, if the general population discovers that we're real, they'll panic and start killing us. In their, fear they will hunt us to extinction."

"Sadly, he's right, folks," sighed Jillian. "Derek expressed some of the same fears when I saw him."

Igor sat beside her and gave her a gentle smile. "So, you saw him, spoke with him?"

"Yes."

"But he wouldn't return with you. He's still not confident in his ability to control the change?"

"Yes."

"Tell me, what do you know of the accident that triggered the change for him?"

"Well, the horse was tangled up in the barbed wire, it was down and frightened. I went for help and when I got back Derek was gone, so was the horse. Derek's clothes were still there, all covered in green dust."

"Da, the green shit. Was it there before, when both man and horse were there?"

"No. I have no idea how it got there."

"Was there a stone near the trapped horse, a green stone?"

"I don't know, let me think a minute. Yes, I think there was at that. Why?"

"That causes the change," said Rhonda. "First you need an animal, angry or frightened, lots of adrenaline, same for the human in close proximity. The stone then has to be triggered to explode. When that happens the radiation from the stone blends the human and animal.

"Something set that stone off, and that's what happened to your lover. Now, having said all that, there's a lot more you need to know about him as he is now, things he needs to know as well."

"Like what? Will he ever be able to control the change?"

"Sure, easily. You said you saw him, was he completely human then?"

"Yes, but he changed back into the horse. He tried not to, but he couldn't stop it."

"When I was first changed it was months before I could change back," said Rhonda. "Even then, I had no real control. These people helped me to master the change, and they'll help your guy, too."

"So, you're saying he'll be able to lead a normal life?"

"Yes and no. It's a bit complicated."

"Okay, explain it to me."

Rhonda relaxed back in the chair beside Jillian and patted her hand. "All right, I'll give it a shot. First, there are things you should know. He's most likely immortal now, super strong, can't be killed, at least not permanently."

"Excuse me?"

"If he gets killed he'll revive, be hungry as hell, and dirt mean for a few days."

"And you know this how?"

"It happened to me, and to others."

"You?"

"I was shot out of the air, dead before I hit the ground. I woke up a few minutes later, mad as hell, and hungry enough to eat a bear raw."

"You're serious. You expect us to believe this."

"It's happened to me, several times," said Marlene. "She speaks the truth."

"So what animal are you?"

Marlene gave Jillian a gentle smile. "Maybe I'll show you one day. Go on, Ronni."

"Okay, back to your boyfriend. He's immortal, and barren."

"Barren, what do you mean, barren?"

"He can't father children, Jill," said Elaine. "Derek will live forever, unchanging, never aging, and he'll have no children. That's the price the shapeshifters pay."

Jillian sat back, shocked at what she'd just heard, but somewhat accepting of it. "But, all the research said the werewolves could create more, by biting someone. Doesn't that make them children of sorts?"

"The werewolves are different," said Rhonda. "They aren't immortal, and they do bear children, not by biting someone, but in the traditional way. They became shapeshifters by some other means, we're not exactly sure how, but we have a theory."

"I don't care about that right now," sighed Jillian. "If that's how it has to be, I'll find a way to cope, it's Derek I love, and I want him back. You said you people would help me."

"We will do that," said Igor. "Please continue, my pretty bird."

"That's all the scary stuff, Jillian," smiled Rhonda. "Now for the other stuff."

"Other stuff?"

"Yes, Derek can have a real life, a human life for the most part, but not here. He'll have to come back with us, so the king can protect him."

"I don't understand. If he learns to control the change, why can't he continue his life here?"

"Because, sooner or later, he could be seen, and then the trouble would start," said Igor. "For many thousands of years my people lived free in the mountains of Russia, long before it was called Russia. However, one day a man discovered us, he watched, he made films, took notes, then sold them.

"The criminals who bought the research came with modern weapons, killed most of our people, and captured many of the young pups. Later, the king came with his warriors and destroyed our captors, setting us free, but we live with the king now, protecting his people, and being sheltered by them. In this world of technology there's no place to hide, you know this.

"We use the latest in technology, as well as our other skills, to keep prying eyes away, and allow us a better life. We would like to take Derek there; you can come too."

"No way, listen to me, no. We can bring him here. It's a horse ranch, no one will think twice about another horse here. He can learn control here, live here, free. No one would know, why would anyone even suspect?"

"Igor, not all live at the castle," said Elaine.

"You speak of Miss Gina and Marko."

"Yes."

"Miss Gina is centuries old, Elaine dear friend, she knows the risks and has the trust of the king."

Jillian sat up straighter at that. "So, it's possible. How does one gain the trust of this king?"

Igor sighed and sank back into a chair. "You go to his castle, speak with him in person, let him judge for himself. I can't help you with that. My task is to bring the horse-man back to the castle."

"And if he won't go?" asked Jill fearfully.

"That's not an option," replied Igor. "Please understand, I have no desire to harm him, none at all. I just want him to come talk to the king. It's not so bad. He's a great guy, our king, you'll like him. Tell her, Elaine."

"He's right," smiled Elaine. "King Harald is a nice man, and Queen Sally is a real sweetheart. Jill, these folks are all good people, you can trust them."

"If you say so."

"Okay, that was unfair, Jill."

"You took the guy in, signed everything over to him, and then he kicked you out. Forgive me if I don't have a lot of faith in the people you trust."

"That hurt," said Elaine, turning away.

Jillian sighed deeply and reached for her sister. "Elaine, I'm sorry, I am. You're right, that was hurtful and mean. Honey, I can see you're happy and in good hands, well cared for. It's just that, it's Derek, and ..."

"Do you want him back or not?" asked Marlene, her voice going hard.

Jillian turned to her and saw her eyes had changed. There was an aura of danger about her now. Jill swallowed hard as she realized this was something else she'd never seen before, a predator of terrible power. "Yes, I want him back," she replied.

"Then stop this resistance and let us help you. Know this, I can make you trust if I want, I can make you do anything at all. Only my respect and love for Elaine is stopping me. The king won't harm you, or your lover, unless you fight us. If you refuse to come, then we'll have to kill you all to keep our existence secret."

As she finished speaking Marlene stood up, her body changing to full vampire killing mode. "You asked what I am. Well this is it, I'm vampire, and I grow annoyed at your resistance." She flexed her long powerful arms and extended her claws.

Jillian shrank away in fear, but Rhonda stepped between them. She looked the vampire in the eye then licked her lips. "Dang, you're sexy when you go all vamp like that."

Startled, Marlene returned to human form and stepped back. "Igor, control your wife. Jesus."

Igor let his shoulders slump. "I have tried so many times, Marlene, but I have failed."

"You like me," grinned Rhonda, as she kissed his cheek. She then turned back to Jillian. "Look, I get that you're frightened, you're protective of your man, and you don't know us. However, as Marlene has so eloquently demonstrated, you're way the hell out of your comfort zone here, and walking on quicksand.

"I get that you want your guy here on this horse ranch. It makes sense to me, it's a natural, and maybe you can convince King Harald to agree to it, but you'll have to come talk to him first. With us, you have a chance, if the government comes, they'll just take him and lock you away someplace dark and deep.

"If the criminals come, they'll kill the lot of you and take the horse-man anyway. So, it's time to stop screwing around and get with the program. You want him back, you were trying to find a way to get him back, we're here to help with that, so stop resisting."

Jillian suddenly burst into tears and was swept into her sister's arms. "Those trust issues run deep, Jillian," Amanda said kindly. "I don't know your family history, but I'd say someone you depended on let you down pretty hard at a delicate time in your formative years."

"Yeah."

"It was me, Amanda," sighed Elaine. "Jill was only fifteen, Mom had died the year before, Dad was trying to drown himself in a bottle, and I ran off with a musician. I thought it was true love, but he was a user and abuser. In the end, Dad was on the street and Jill had to move in with Peg and Merle.

"I don't have a great track record of trusting the right people. Getting this job at the castle is the best thing that ever happened to me. It got me straight, it returned my self-respect, my confidence, and it gave me a life I love.

"Jill, honey, give me one more chance, let these nice folks help you. Look at them, most are shapeshifters themselves. They know and understand some of what Derek will be facing. They can help him; they want to help him."

Jillian sniffed then slowly disentangled herself from her sister's arms. "Okay, I'm sorry. I'll let you guys take over. Just promise to help Derek."

"We will," said Rhonda. "First we locate him, then I'll make contact."

"Excuse me, am I not lead agent here?"

"Of course you are, dear. As I was saying, I'll make contact, give him more information to work with, and try to convince him to come home with us."

"My sweet Lady Hawk ..."

"You're a predator, my big bad wolf. You all are, and he's a horse, a natural prey animal. You'll scare the crap out of him. The hawk is small and not a natural threat. I have a much better chance of getting close to him."

"Why can't I go to him? He knows and trusts me; he'll listen to me."

"All right, Jill," said Igor, "let's try it your way first. You talk to him, try to convince him to come here to the ranch to speak with us. What do you think, my pretty bird?"

"Okay, sounds reasonable. I'll be overhead when you make contact, Jill. If he refuses you, then I'll follow him and make contact, try it my way. Does that work for you?"

Jillian nodded slowly. "Yeah, that makes sense."

"All right then," said Merle. "We have a plan, let's saddle up."

"Saddle up?" asked Igor.

"We can get there a lot faster on horseback than if we have to drive the long way around. What's the matter, Agent Wolf, never ridden a horse before?"

"No. I've eaten a few, but ..."

Seeing the look on Jillian's face, Rhonda slapped Igor on the arm. "He's teasing, Jill. Just teasing. Come on, you can make fun of him when he's in the saddle."

"Sweet Ronni, leave the wolf some dignity." Rhonda just took his arm then winked at Jillian.

They all went to the corral and Merle called in the horses. They were skittish, as they could sense the predators. It took Merle a while to get the wolves and vampire mounted and their horses calmed. Peggy offered the reins to Rhonda, but she laughed and leaped toward the sky. A few beats of strong wings and she was floating lazily overhead.

The others rode out, Merle muttering about it being like a trail ride for tourists. Peggy hushed him, and they continued over the hills, arriving late in the day. There was nothing, no horses to be seen and the fence was still broken.

"This is all wrong," said Jill. "He said he'd stay close."

"No horses have been here for days," said Branimir. "The scent is old."

"There were men, though," said Igor. "But that was days ago as well. See, here are the marks on the road. It looks like a big truck was here."

"No, oh god, no," moaned Jill, as she leaped from the saddle and began to inspect the ground.

"Talk to me, Miss Jillian."

"Rustlers, Igor. There are men with trucks that capture wild horses and sell them for dog food. Oh god, if they've got him he could be dead by now."

"Maybe, but only for a few minutes," said Igor, as he raised his arm and gave a piercing whistle.

The hawk dropped from the sky and transformed into Rhonda as it neared the ground. What is it, lover?"

"There was a truck here, and since then, no horses. They may have been taken. Larise and Amanda will see about tracking that down. Bran and I will poke around and see if we can discover more. You, my beloved Lady Hawk, must fly. The horses may have escaped, and if they did, you must find them."

Rhonda nodded and turned to Jillian. "If they escaped, where would they go?"

"Probably that way, northwest. There's some good horse friendly hill country about a week's walk from here."

"Won't take me that long. I'll go have a look." She gave Igor a searing kiss then leaped into the sky, flying off to the northwest.

"Ow! Dammit woman." Igor turned to see Peggy shaking a finger at Merle, who was rubbing his arm.

"She's quite an eyeful, my Lady Hawk, is she not?" grinned Igor.

"I can't help it," grumbled Merle. "She keeps running around here stark naked. I'm only human. Sorry about that."

"She is pleasant to look at, and I have no objections. If she does, she'll let you know. It's the way of the shapeshifter. When we shift, we appear naked. Now, Bran and I need to check this place out thoroughly. Won't be long." With that, both men shimmered into the huge dire wolves.

They snuffled about for some time then, as though driven by a single mind, they set out to the northwest. "Well, you can put your mind at rest, Jillian," said Larise, as she dismounted and gathered up their clothes. "The rustlers didn't get your horses."

"How can you know that?"

"Because my boss and my husband just went northwest at a dead run. They're on the scent, so, the horses got away."

"What'll they do?" asked Peggy.

"They'll track them down. Dr. Stockman will find them first, but Bran and Igor won't be too far behind. They'll bring Derek to us. Up to you folks, you can follow the wolves, or we can go back to the ranch for a night's sleep. Me, I'm for going back, then I have to check in with the local law about the rustlers."

"The rustlers? They didn't get Derek, why do we care?"

"Igor said for me to track them down, so that's what I'll do. They may have seen him change, we have to know and deal with it if they did."

"Deal with it?"

"Yes, deal with it," said Marlene.

"Well, to hell with it, I don't care about that, I'm going after Derek." With that Jillian urged her horse away.

"She'll need protection, Marlene."

"I know. Toss you for it, Larise."

"Sorry girl, but you can see in the dark, I can't."

"Dammit, I haven't been on a horse in fifty years. If I get saddle sores, Larise Parker, you're in deep trouble." Marlene urged her horse after Jillian.

"She actually looks pretty comfortable in the saddle," mused Peggy.

"She is," grinned Amanda. "Marlene is several centuries old, and well acquainted with a saddle. However, she'd prefer a limo. Come on folks, let's go back to the ranch. We can find a hotel and get a good night's sleep."

"We've got plenty of room at the ranch," said Peggy. "You can bunk with us. Come on, it's getting dark." With that, they rode away.

Wild Horses

While Jillian was being introduced to the King's agents, Derek was deep in the hill country. After he'd smashed the drone he took the herd far away. He understood the danger modern technology represented to the horses. They were wild things, children of the winds, racers across time, a living part of the natural world. He had to keep them safe.

The small, sheltered, valley he'd chosen as their haven was lush with grass and had a natural spring-fed pool of water. The place was perfect for horses to hide out. The herd grazed contentedly nearby, fully trusting the red stallion to keep them safe. For his part, he grazed near the valley mouth where he could easily keep watch for enemies.

For two days they stayed in the sheltering valley, eating and drinking their fill. On the third day his senses went on full alert. There was nothing moving that he could see, but every instinct he had was screaming of danger. Still, no danger presented itself, just the hawk far overhead, circling to the left.

Trusting the horse's instincts, he began to call the herd out of the valley. He turned them northwest again, then set out at a gallop, the herd streaming out behind him. By nightfall the herd was out on the plains under a star filled sky. The stallion set himself to watch through the night. Nothing could approach without his knowledge.

The next day, he let the herd graze. They were tired; he'd been pushing too hard. Taking his time, he searched out water and led them to it. The day was well along before he noticed the hawk again, high above, circling to the left. For some reason it made him nervous, and he still sensed danger following.

Settling the herd down for the night beside the waterhole, he found a hillock to watch from. He slept little that night, and close to dawn he succumbed to his fatigue.

The sun was up when he awakened shivering, the air cold against his bare skin. Derek rubbed his hands over his face then looked up. There was a naked woman sitting on a rock, smiling at him. "You're naked."

"Yes I am," she grinned. "Like what you see?" He blushed deeply and looked away. "By the way, I could mention that you're naked as well." That didn't help his embarrassment any, and her silvery laughter floated lightly on the air.

"It's weird, isn't it, and disconcerting as hell the first few times," she went on.

"Huh? What do you mean?"

"The first few times you change back to yourself and realize you're buck naked."

"Change back?"

"From the animal; you're a were-horse, and at first, you'll spend most of your time in horse form, but as you begin to master the change, you'll be able to spend more time as human. Eventually, you'll be able to change back and forth instantly whenever you like."

"How do you know all this? How do you know what I am?"

"There's been a hawk watching you for a couple of days, right?"

"Yes. That was you?"

"You don't believe me? Watch." With that she leaped skyward, climbed high then plummeted toward the ground. She leveled off her dive, turning it into a gentle glide, then transformed in mid flight to land right beside the stone she'd sat on before. "Convinced?"

Derek just stared at her for a few moments before he found his voice. "So, I'm not the only one?"

"Nope. I know a few more, and they'd love to meet you, help you gain full control of the change." He just stared at her incredulously. "Come on, Derek, what'd ya say? Come with me and meet the gang?"

He still wasn't sure. This was all too unbelievable. "Just who are you?"

She smiled and stood up. "Dr. Rhonda Stockman, veterinarian, at your service, Mr. Wheeler. They call me the Lady Hawk."

"How do you know my name?"

"Jill's been frantic to get help for you. Her sister works for our employer, and he sent us to help you."

"I don't need any help."

She sighed and sat back down. "Look, Derek, there's a lot you don't yet know about what's happened to you, what you are now. You do need our help, and you need to remain out of the knowledge of regular humans."

"I already had that part figured out."

"I'm sure you have an idea what will happen if the government gets their hands on you."

"I can Imagine."

"Your fate if the criminal element gets hold of you would be worse. There really is only one safe haven."

"And where is that?"

"With the king. Harald Eldredsson is the king of all non-humans. He's a good man and he's offered you protection and assistance, sanctuary."

"Why?"

"Several reasons. One, he wants to keep you out of the public eye. Two, your woman is sister to a friend of his. Three, you're non-human, and as such, you're one of his people. He wants to protect you."

"What if I don't want to be one of his people."

"Use your head. He has to keep his people out of the public eye. If you refuse to cooperate, what choice do you leave him?"

"Are you saying he'd kill me?"

"Yes. They're almost here, Derek. God, you're as stubborn as Jillian. Use your head, man, stop fighting us."

"What? Wait, what do you mean, they're almost here?"

"My husband and his pack mate. They're werewolves, dire wolves from a bygone age. They're big, fast, tough, and utterly relentless. Also, they can be somewhat scary, that's why I came on ahead to talk to you first.

"Don't do it. I can see it in your eyes, but if you run from these guys, they'll hunt you down and finish you. Jillian, too."

"What??? They'd kill her? What the hell did she do?"

"She knows, Derek. Listen to me now, the king's a reasonable man. Come with us, hear what he has to say. If you decide to stay with us, Jill can stay too. We wouldn't separate you."

"Jesus, woman."

"Just sit down and relax, Igor is near, I can sense him. Don't try to run."

"My herd ..."

"I can see a young stallion there, leave the herd to him. You've brought them to a place of safety, leave them to him."

"I ... no, I ..."

"You can't."

"What? I can't what?"

"Breed the mares. Derek, you're a shapeshifter now, you're immortal, and you're barren. That's the price we pay."

"What do you mean, immortal?"

"I mean you'll live forever, never age, never grow old. The world will change around you, but you'll always be the same as you are now. The same physical man, same horse, never changing. Your lover will grow old before your eyes, your friends, and all that you know will pass away, but you will remain as you are."

"Holy shit," he breathed, as he sank back onto the ground. "Jesus woman, you paint a lonely existence."

"It's what we both face, Derek Wheeler, you and I."

"Wait, did you say barren?"

"I did. As a man you will father no children, and as a stallion you will sire no foals."

"That means that you ..."

"Will bear no children. My husband's line will perish with him, and the line of another will lead the pack. We don't get a choice, Derek, we just get to live with it."

"I can't believe all this, I just can't."

"It's a lot to take in all at once, I know. Come on, brother, come back with me, accept the help. It'll be fun. Come on, you know you want to."

"All right, I ... shit, losing control ..." Slowly he shimmered back into the big red stallion.

The horse stood still as the woman approached and lightly stroked his neck. "Come on, let's go meet the boys." With a snort of agreement, the horse knelt for her to mount.

THE TWO DIRE WOLVES loped along at a pace that easily ate the miles. The scent of the horse was strong on the breeze now, mixed with the sweet scent of the Lady Hawk. They stopped, their tongues lolling as they saw the horse top the rise with a naked woman on its back. Igor morphed back into the man while Bran just laid down to rest.

"So, my pretty bird, this is where I find you, astride another man while I'm on the hunt."

"Jealousy will get you nowhere, my lover," she laughed, as she hopped down and kissed him deeply. "I didn't want you two savages to eat him before I could stop you."

"Ah-huh."

"Stop it, Igor." She was laughing, and he was grinning at her.

"So, you are Derek Wheeler? Yes?"

The horse tossed its head. "I believe your Jill is not too far behind us. Shall we go back then?"

Igor shifted back into the wolf again, causing the horse to shy away, but Rhonda leaped nimbly to his back and he settled down. The two wolves turned and led the way, the horse and rider close behind.

Long hours passed before they caught sight of the riders in the distance. As they drew closer, the stallion caught Jillian's scent and called out to her. Jillian urged her horse to greater speed as she went to him. She leaped from the saddle and threw her arms around the stallion's neck.

"Oh god, Derek. Honey, these folks say they can help us. They want us to go with them."

Rhonda slid off the horse's back. "He knows, Jillian, he came of his own free will. It's getting late, we should find a place to camp for the night. Once he relaxes he may be able to change back."

"Over this way. There's a spring out of the wind. I camped there when I was hunting for him." Jillian led the way and they soon set up camp.

Far away the queen sighed and opened her eyes, reaching for the king's hand. "It's begun, Harald. Rhonda has met the were-horse."

"So now we wait," he sighed, as he gently pulled her closer.

"Now we wait."

Horse Thieves

Marlene was grumbling as she started the fire. Rhonda's head came up at that. "Marlene?"

"I'm okay, but starting to get hungry."

"Want me to go up and scout for you?"

Marlene gave a curt nod and Rhonda leaped skyward. "When she makes a tight circle to the left your prey will be beneath her," grinned Igor. Marlene nodded then trotted off in the direction the Lady Hawk and taken.

"What's going on?" asked Jillian.

"Marlene is vampire," said Igor. "She can go many days without feeding, but this she has done already. My Lady Hawk will spy out the prey and the vampire will feed. All is well."

"What sort of prey?"

"Animal, most likely," he replied. "However, if fortune smiles and a human is near ..."

"She's going to kill someone?"

"Relax, Miss Marlene won't kill anyone, just feed. A dead body drained of blood is hard to explain, but a weak and sickly human is not. She will feed, but not kill."

"God, this is all so surreal. Werewolves, shapeshifters, vampires ..."

"All stories to frighten children, yeah?" grinned Igor.

"Yeah. I suppose that's you guys at work."

"Da, or those like us."

"So, you're Russian?"

"I was born there, yes. The first language I learned was an ancient dialect of Russian spoken only by my people. Once taken slave, we learned some Russian, but mostly English because America is where Krebs wanted us to be working as assassins. Once the king and his American allies set us free he brought us here, and so here we are."

"You think of yourselves as Americans now?"

"No, we're King Harald's people. We live in America for now, but who knows where we'll be in the future."

"How many of you are there?"

"Many, and by human standards, not so many at all. Some are here, others in Europe, and there may be others I know nothing about."

"Are there many shapeshifters?"

"Only a few. Of the shapeshifters the wolves are most numerous, then the vampires, I know of one werebear, one were-hawk, one were-mouse ..."

"A mouse?"

"Da," chuckled Igor. "A woman, most beautiful, was in an accident much like your Derek. It was I who caught her and convinced her to trust us, to come to the castle and learn control of the change. She got me in all kinds of trouble."

"She did?" chuckled Branimir. "You did that all by yourself."

"Shut up, Bran."

Jillian smiled in spite of her fears. She was starting to like these guys. "Oh, there's a story there. Come on, Bran, tell me a story."

"I wasn't there, but I was told Igor caught her, she was trapped part way through the change, not woman and not mouse. Igor held her, called her his beautiful girl, his brave little mouse."

"Really?"

"Da, the Lady Hawk didn't like that," grinned Branimir. "She'd already chosen him for herself."

"Shut up, Bran. It wasn't like that. I wanted to protect her, make her feel safe so we could help her." Igor chuckled at the memory. "Da, I was being protective, and it lost something in the translation. Sweet Ronni and I had not yet bonded, but we both knew we were meant for each other. I had some serious sucking up to do."

Jill was smiling at him. "I'll just bet. She sure is a fierce one."

"Da, wild as a hawk."

"You like it."

"Yes, I do. Ah, she's returning."

The call of the hawk was soon followed by Rhonda who transformed and dropped into Igor's arms. "Hey, handsome, did you miss me?"

"I always miss you when you're not with me, my pretty bird."

"Good answer," she grinned as she kissed his cheek. "Jill, we may have a small problem."

"Oh?"

"We found what we believe to be your rustlers."

"Oh crap. Where's Marlene?"

"Having dinner and seeing what she can learn about these people. She should be back soon."

Suddenly the stallion shimmered back into Derek Wheeler. "We need to get out of here."

"Why?" asked Igor.

"Rustlers are extremely dangerous. We need to ..."

"Relax and cuddle your girl," said Rhonda. "That's what you need to do. Yes, those people may be dangerous but, as they say, you ain't seen nothin' yet. Derek, our people will keep you safe. You snuggle up to Jill now, and we'll wait for Marlene to return, see what she's learned."

Jillian had a blanket around her shoulders and she opened it to invite Derek in to share the warmth. Warily, he joined her, and she wrapped the blanket tightly around them both and cuddled him to her. He sighed and fairly melted into her arms.

Igor caught Bran's eye and motioned toward Derek. Bran nodded and shifted his weight closer to the small fire. "So, Derek, tell me what it's like for you."

"Like?"

"Da. Igor and I are children of the forests. We grew up among the trees. What's it like to run across the wide-open lands?"

Derek's smile was almost wistful. "It's amazing, like nothing I could have imagined before. That body is so strong, powerful. As the horse, I feel like I can outrun anything. I can race the wind, and be as hard to catch.

"I can sense when danger is near, and at a single call the herd will turn as one to follow me. I can head out into the open and just run, nothing can catch me. What about you? What's it like to go wolf?"

Branimir chuckled. "Different. As wolf, my senses are strong, my instincts keen. I know when prey is near, or another wolf. I look to my alpha, to see what we do next. Do we hunt? Track? Chase? Fight? What?"

"Yeah, I guess you guys are predators, I'm not, I'm prey. So, what's the most dangerous prey you've ever tackled?"

Bran looked to be lost in thought. He glanced up at Igor who gave him the nod to continue. "It was last fall. We faced something that shouldn't exist, a wrong thing created by a mad vampire. It was a carue, a bull elk made into a vampire, terribly strong and savage, with amazing healing abilities. It changed from the elk into a half elk-half man as we fought.

"I was getting my ass kicked when Igor arrived and saved me."

"Ah, you didn't need saving, you'd already defeated the carue."

"Bullshit," chuckled Bran. "It took both of us to bring it down."

"Da," agreed Igor. "Damn, that thing was hard to kill."

"Tell me about the rustlers," said Bran.

"Nice change of subject, Slick," grinned Jillian. "Okay, the rustlers, they capture wild horses then sell them to the slaughterhouses that make dog food. The horses in this area are protected, in theory, but rustlers are hard to catch, they carry guns, and they're willing to use them."

"Yeah, and they use modern tech to help them," said Derek. "They came at my herd with a drone, trying to drive us back to the trap."

"What happen?" asked Bran.

"It dropped low enough for me to get a good kick at it. One dead drone, but it was close. Several times the herd turned, and I had to call them back, away from the trap. I ..." Marlene re-entered the camp, licking her lips. She settled to the ground beside Bran.

"So, did I miss anything good while I was out having dinner?"

"No, we were just waiting for you to get back before we started the party."

"Good answer, Bran," grinned Marlene, nudging him with a shoulder. "Larise has you well trained."

"That'll cost you."

"Maybe later," she said, suddenly leaping back to her feet. "They're coming."

"Take cover," said Igor, as he and Branimir transformed and bolted out of sight. The Lady Hawk was already in the air and the stallion racing away as the rustlers entered the now empty camp.

The leader's voice carried easily to Jillian. "They can't be far, find them. Catch the women alive, they could be worth a fortune." The armed men spread out, searching the area with powerful flashlights. It wasn't long before a light found Jill. She was tackled to the ground, but her attacker was soon ripped off her. He screamed in terror as the vampire sank her fangs into his neck.

Another light appeared and lit up the man in the vampire's deadly embrace. Three shots rang out, the bullets piercing the body of her victim. Marlene dropped him and vanished into the gloom. The gunman turned his attention to Jill, but was tackled and ripped apart by a huge wolf.

Igor appeared,. standing over the dead body. "Jillian, are you okay?"
Eyes wide with fear, she still managed to find her voice. "Yes."

"Hide." He went wolf again and vanished into the darkness. There were more screams in the night as the wolves and vampire dispatched the rustlers, and then silence fell.

Marlene suddenly appeared beside Jillian, nearly causing her to faint from fear. This wasn't the small pixie with the red hair and freckles, but Marlene in full killing mode. This creature was taller, had exceptionally long muscular arms, tipped with powerful looking clawed hands, and a cat-like face with long fangs protruding from her upper jaw.

The vampire sniffed the air, listened intently for a moment, and then morphed back into the girl. "Jillian, are you all right?"

"What? Oh, yeah, I'm good. Is it over?"

"I believe it may be. I'll stay with you now, until Igor gives the all-clear."

A few moments later the Hawk swooped in and transformed. "It's over, you guys okay?"

"We're good, Ronni. The boys all right?"

"Oh yeah, they're fine. Derek lit out like the devil himself was on his tail, the guys went after him. Look, you two find your horses then get out of here. This'll look like a bunch of rustlers bumped into a wolf pack and it all went bad. I'll fly ahead and find Derek before the guys do."

Jillian gave her a puzzled look. "They're predators, Jill, and they're on the hunt. He'll catch their scent, then run halfway to Canada with them on his trail. I'll get out in front of him and settle him down before they catch up." She sighed and gave Jillian a gentle hug.

"He's more than half horse right now, Jill, running on the horse's instincts. It takes time to get past that, become more human again. For now, he'll react better to me because I'm no threat, not a natural predator. Once I can help him transform, we'll wait for Igor, and then make a plan.

"You guys get back to your friend's ranch so Larise can run interference for you after you inform the police about the rustlers."

"It's okay, Ronni, I'll get her back safely. You go look after your boys." Rhonda nodded then leaped into the air and flew away.

"Her boys?"

"Igor's the pack alpha," said Marlene. "He dotes on Ronni, she bosses them all around like a mother hen, and they all love it. Looks like she's taken Derek under her wing as well. That's a good sign."

"It is? Why?"

"Ronni's a veterinarian, loves animals, and is fiercely protective. Igor's pack will obey her and defend her to the death. Derek will get spoiled rotten once he loses that natural fear of them."

"Okay, if you say so. Can I ask you something?"

"What was that I turned into?"

"Yeah, is it okay to ask? Was that the full vampire?"

"Sure, you can ask. That was the vampire's killing mode, the half-tiger. In that form I'm a lot stronger, faster, my reflexes and senses, keener. We vampires can only become the half-tiger. Only Ella, the original vampire, can fully become the saber-toothed tigress. You haven't seen anything truly scary until you've seen Ella go on the warpath. Come on now, we've got horses to find and saddle."

"Huh? Oh yeah. They won't be far."

"You sure? Igor and Bran went full wolf. I'll bet those horses put a bit of distance between themselves and those guys."

"Shit, you're probably right. Ah well, sun's coming up now, let's get started. I wonder which way they went."

"That way. I can smell them."

"You can? Now that's handy."

Marlene was chuckling as they set out to catch the horses.

BACK AT THE RUSTLER'S truck, two nervous people waited for the men who would never return. "Damn it, Bill, I don't like this. We shouldn't be here at all."

"I don't care, Mona, I want that herd gone. I can't afford to keep mending that fence."

"But, you heard the gunfire last night."

"They were probably trying to run that herd back here to the truck. Look, all we have to do is tend the trap, wave these rags around to chase the horses into the truck then we get paid and that damned herd is gone."

"Shouldn't they be back by now?" she asked nervously. "These guys don't like to be out in the broad daylight."

Shading his eyes, he gazed off toward the horizon. "Yeah, maybe."

"We should take off."

"We can't, Mona, not now. If they come back and we're not here to catch the horses, they'll come after us. Honey, we don't want these men on our trail. We don't."

"Well, I don't like it, I've got a bad feeling."

"Yeah, me too. Look, do you want me to take that last saddle pony and go look for them?"

"I'd rather run, but yeah, maybe you should." He nodded then saddled up the horse and rode out in the direction taken by his friends the night before. He found the bodies an hour later. He returned to his wife at a gallop.

"Start the jeep," he shouted, as he leaped from the saddle and swiftly stripped it off the horse. He tossed it aside, pulled off the halter then slapped the horse on the rump to start it running away. "Go, go, go," he urged, as he jumped into the passenger's seat.

"What happened?" she asked, as she spun out of the loose dirt and onto the hard-packed road.

"Dunno, but they're all dead. Mona, it looked like they'd been torn apart by wolves."

"Wolves? We heard gun fire last night."

"Just telling you what I saw. They'd been ripped apart, there was wolf sign everywhere, and they were all dead. Jesus."

"What'll we do, Bill?"

"We go home, we were there all weekend."

"What if they find our fingerprints on those trucks."

"Doesn't prove a thing. We were home. Those guys came by, wanting to buy old horses for dog food. We had nothing for them, so they drove away."

"Dammit, Bill, this all started when you shot at that conservation man. Everything's gone to hell since then." He didn't try to argue any further. She was right.

Meanwhile, Back at the Ranch

While Rhonda and the wolves tracked down the wild stallion, Larise and Amanda paid a visit to the local sheriff. Larise flashed her old badge and he was willing to share what he had on the case. "Agent Parker, can you tell me why the feds have such an interest in this case?"

"Between you and me, Sheriff, a friend called in a favor from somebody in a higher pay grade than me. You know how it is."

"Indeed I do. Right now I've got the mayor wanting me to give something else priority. I'm more than happy to hand this one over. Actually, I'm surprised that gal isn't here with you, cracking the whip."

"You mean Jillian Arbend? She's out on horseback with her own search party. Another agent is with her. They can have the saddle sores; I took the leg work in town. So, there was no reason or indication that he might just take off?"

"None anybody knew of. The guy was all about saving the wild horses. Probably got a cowboy fixation or something. The thing I can't figure out is why his clothes were left there?"

"Can you think of a better way to confuse the issue?"

"No, I guess not. So you think this guy just took off, for some reason?"

"It's the best explanation I can think of. I'm sure he didn't magically turn into a bird and fly away. He had somebody there to help him, left a bunch of confusion behind, then disappeared."

59

"Makes sense to me, but why the hell do that, leave his woman hanging like that?"

"A few years ago, Sheriff," said Amanda, "I worked with a woman in similar circumstances. We eventually learned her husband was transsexual, the wife hated the idea of it, so one day he just disappeared. We eventually found him, but by then he was a she."

"You're a shrink, right? You think this guy ..."

"Sheriff, I'm just saying there are plenty of reasons a person could have for wanting to disappear. I think we'll approach the case as though that's what most likely happened. As my colleague said, he couldn't have turned into a bird and just flown away. No, this bird has flown, but I'm sure he used wheels to do it."

"Yeah. I suggested something like that, but Ms. Arbend didn't take it well. All right, Agent Parker, it's all yours now, and welcome to it. Good luck."

"Thanks, Sheriff. I think," chuckled Larise, as she accepted the file from his hand and turned to the door.

Once back in their car Larise grinned at Amanda. "Woman, remind me to never play poker with you."

"Me? You were pretty darn convincing yourself."

"Thank you, thank you. I loved the transsexual story. I wouldn't try that one with a polygraph though."

"That one would pass the polygraph. We actually worked that case. Okay, here's the address of the people who own the fence that was broken down. I think we should interview them, make certain they didn't see anything they shouldn't."

Larise programmed the address into the GPS and they drove away. The place turned out to be a small cattle ranch that had seen better days. The owners weren't home, so they decided to return later. They went back to the ranch where Elaine had stayed with her friends.

"So, how'd it go with the sheriff?" asked Merle, as they entered the door.

"All good there," said Larise. "He was more than happy to hand over the case to us. Any word from the others?"

"No, and I wish they'd call," said Peggy.

"Peg, honey," smiled Elaine, "these folks don't have a lot of pockets, if you get what I mean."

"Yeah, well, Jill does, and you don't often see her without that phone in her hand." Just then her phone buzzed. She looked down at it, then sighed with relief. "On our way back. Success."

"Looks like they found him," said Merle.

"That's good news," said Larise. "The day's getting late, so I think we'll wait until tomorrow to see if we can track down that rancher."

"What rancher is that?" asked Merle.

"The man who owns the fence that was broken down near where Derek disappeared. I want to make certain he hasn't seen anything he shouldn't."

"You be careful of that man, girl. He's got a temper, and he's been known to get nasty."

"I'll bear that in mind," replied Larise, "but don't worry about me. I've seen nasty, and I doubt that rancher could hold a candle to it."

"Perhaps you should wait until you can take Marlene with you, just in case," said Amanda. "It'll be far less suspicious if she puts the compulsion on him rather than if you shoot him."

Larise laughed at that. "Good point. All right, we wait. Any idea what we should be doing while we wait?"

"Ella always says, when there's nothing to do but wait, you should rest and eat."

"That's my cue to get in the kitchen," smiled Peggy.

NEXT MORNING THEY WERE all up early, gathered around the breakfast table when Amanda spoke. "I think we should be looking to buy a horse trailer to tow behind Jillian's truck. If Derek hasn't gained full control of the change I don't want him in the plane with me when he loses it."

"Yeah, that makes sense," replied Larise. "So, you think she'll have to drive him across the country?"

"I do, and I think Igor will want to go along."

"He will. He'll stay with Derek until he's been delivered to the king. All right, you'll have to take the plane back, Bran and I may be able to go with you, I expect Elaine will want to stay with her sister, and Igor will want Marlene with him just in case."

"All speculation at the moment," sighed Amanda.

"Actually, I should return to the castle with you," said Elaine. "I've already been away from my post too long."

"Getting twitchy, girl?" grinned Larise.

"You know me too well," sighed Elaine, as she stepped into Larise's arms and hugged her.

"It's all right, sweet sister, I've got you. They're on the way back now, it won't be too much longer. You can go back with Amanda when she returns the plane."

"Thank you, Larise," sighed Elaine, as she hugged Larise tightly then released her. "I'll make that tea for you now."

Puzzled, Peggy and Merle gave each other a questioning look then turned to Amanda. "What just happened?"

"People, Elaine and Larise have become close friends in recent months, they watch out for each other. Elaine is the house master at the castle. That means that she's the person who directs all the household staff. There's a reason for this, she's psychic. Our amazing Elaine knows what you want before you do, and usually has it waiting when you're ready.

"She's invaluable to Mr. Eldredsson, and the rest of us. She also gets unnerved when away from the castle for too long."

"Peg, you know what I was like before, when I was growing up, and after I ran away at sixteen. I was confused, made a lot of bad choices, then finally got lucky. That job makes me feel safe, whole, and appreciated. I belong there, I can function there, and I feel that this is what I was meant to do with my life. I'm well paid, well supported, appreciated, and I feel fulfilled."

"What about a man, children, things like that? They can be fulfilling too, honey," said Peggy.

"I know," smiled Elaine, a twinkle in her eye. "There's a gentleman at the castle who's been giving me the eye. I think it might just be the right time to encourage him a bit."

"Alas, poor Jimmy," chuckled Larise. "He doesn't stand a chance. He ..." Larise stopped speaking, Peggy was staring at her phone again. "Peggy, what is it?"

"They've been hit by rustlers. Jill and that Marlene girl are on their way back. Derek took off, the vet and the two men are going after him."

"Shit, that can't be good. What do you mean, rustlers?"

"Horse thieves. They steal the wild horses and sell them for dog food. They're bad people, dangerous, best avoided if possible."

"Did she say if anyone was hurt?" asked Merle.

"If they attacked our people, they're probably all dead; the rustlers, I mean," said Amanda. "Looks like we'll have more damage control to do, Larise."

"Yeah, looks like. I knew it was too easy. Look, Elaine's getting stressed. When they get here, I'll keep Marlene with me, you take Elaine back to the castle. We're far enough along now, she can go back."

"Far enough along?" asked Merle.

"I came for Jill, and to help her to trust these people," said Elaine. "The king thought it would be best for Jill if she could see a friendly face at first. That's done now, and she's accepted our help. Now I need to get back and prepare a place for her."

"A place for her?"

"To live. She'll want to stay with Derek. I'll get to have my baby sister near, get to make amends for past troubles. I'm a bit excited at the chance to get to know the woman she's become."

"Yeah, well, just don't run off until she gets here."

"Oh, Peg, no, I won't do that to her again. Besides, nobody's going anywhere until Igor gets back."

"Igor?"

"He's team leader on this, we'll give him our thoughts, our findings, and opinions, then he'll make the decisions. I do hope he'll let me go back early."

"He will, Elaine, he will," said Amanda, as she patted Elaine's hand.

"You sound pretty certain."

"I am. Igor protects his pack above all else. You're his now, one of his pack as long as this job takes. He'll do whatever is best for you as long as it doesn't compromise the operation."

Elaine sighed. "Of course, you're right, Igor's the ultimate alpha. I don't mean to be so messed up. I don't."

"You're fine, girl. As soon as he gets back I'll ask him about getting the plane back to the Lair. I'll need a co-pilot."

Elaine turned to fully face Amanda. "So that's it. You guys are pretty sneaky, and I do love you for it."

"Okay, what did we miss this time?"

"Peg, Amanda is the best psychiatrist in the business. Igor said he wanted her along to help with Jill and Derek, but I'm getting the sense she's actually here for me, is that right?"

Amanda chuckled and patted her hand again. "Busted. Yes, my dear Elaine, Igor needed a pilot, but had you not accompanied us, he would have sent me back with the plane as soon as we touched down. Marlene could have easily handled any resistance he might have encountered."

"So I'm one of his pack now?"

"As he sees it, yes, besides, he also sees you as a friend."

"Sounds like an amazing guy," said Peggy. "Is he married?"

"He is amazing, Peg," said Elaine, "and yes, he's married, to the Lady Hawk, remember?"

"Oh yeah, the one that keep walking around naked."

"Yeah, that one," grinned Larise.

"Well, this is getting dangerous," said Merle, as he rose from the table. "I think I'll go out and prepare a stall for Derek. Maybe that old horse trailer of ours would do the trick for these folks. I'll check the tires, get it ready for the road." All four women were grinning at him as he walked out, red-faced.

IT WAS NEARLY DARK when Jill and Marlene arrived, tired and dusty. Merle helped them unsaddle and rub down the horses, then led them inside. "Marlene, what happened?" asked Larise, as they entered.

"Ronni found them about a mile from our camp. I was getting hungry, so she went scouting for me. I spotted the guard well away from their trucks and camp, so I took him down, then put the compulsion on him. From there I went back to our camp. Done deal, right?

"Not so much. Someone from their camp must have seen me leaving. Next thing you know they're in the camp, looking to capture the women and kill the men. Derek took off like a shot. The rest of us finished them off, made it look like wolf kill, or as best we could.

"Ronni sent Jill and me back here while she went after Derek. Igor and Bran were already on his trail, but she figured that, as panicked as he was, he'd run forever with the wolf scent behind him. She wanted to get out in front of him, settle him down before the boys catch up.

"So, how'd you guys make out?"

"We had it mapped and wrapped," sighed Larise, "until you guys started slaughtering rustlers."

"Oh fuck," sighed Marlene, as she sank back into the chair into which she had settled. "Yeah, looks like you and I will be on damage control."

"That was my thought," replied Larise. "We can leave Elaine and Amanda here while we go mess with the sheriff."

At that, Marlene sat up straight and turned to take a hard look at Elaine. The girl didn't make eye-contact. *Elaine, hear me. You're with friends, in the arms of a loving family. You are safe and loved here. You're at peace, relaxed, and content.*

Elaine sighed and looked up, smiling. "Marlene, thank you for that."

"Feeling better now?"

"Much."

"Awesome." Marlene settled back into the chair. "I'm thinking that plane should go back to the Lair as soon as possible, this evening would be good. Amanda will need a co-pilot. That's a job for Elaine, don't you think?"

"I do," grinned Larise, "but shouldn't we wait for Igor to return first? It's his decision, after all."

"Up to you, but I wouldn't wait."

"I can't, Marlene. I ran out on Jill once before; I need to make sure she understands before I leave."

"Elaine, when we walked through that door, you were fidgeting just like you used to," sighed Jill. "Honey, what Marlene just did was to help you keep it together, right?"

"Yes it was, honey, but I'm okay now."

Jillian took her sister's hands in her own and gazed into her eyes. "You go on, I'll be fine. Honey, I can't go on that plane anyway. Derek will need to travel in a horse trailer, and I'll need to be right there with him. We'll only be a week or so behind you. It'll be okay."

"Jill, are you sure?"

"I'm sure. Look, I'll have Marlene to keep an eye on me, I'll be fine. I can see that you need to get back to where you feel safe. You go on ahead, make sure I've got a place to go to."

"Jill ..."

"It's okay, Elaine. I know you're not running out on me. I know that. Honey, I was completely messed up, terrified, in deep trouble, and you left your safe place to come to me, to bring help for me. I know you love me, and I love you, my sister. You go on ahead, and I'll come to you as soon as I can. Your friends will protect me until I get there, okay?"

Elaine nodded her head, relief clear in her voice as she spoke. "Okay." The vampire's compulsion could keep her on an even keel, but she still felt a sense of relief at the thought of returning to the castle.

"Go on now," said Jillian. "Pack your gear and git." Elaine kissed her cheek and fled the room.

"That was well done," smiled Amanda.

"You weren't here for me at all, were you, Lady Shrink? You were here to help Elaine all along."

"Yes."

"Take her home where she'll feel safe. I'll get there as soon as I can."

"Looks like you've had a change of heart," said Larise.

"I have," sighed Jillian. "Marlene saved my life twice over. She's scary as hell when she goes full vampire, and that Lady Hawk is something else again, so are the wolves. Look, if this is the quality of people who will be watching out for, and helping, Derek, I want that. I'll do everything in my power to make it happen."

Larise nodded then relaxed. There was nothing more to do until Igor returned.

Horse Sense

The big red horse slowed to a trot, his sides heaving as he dragged deep lungsful of air into his body. The sweat foamed on him, and his eyes were nearly glazed over. He was well out in the open, and as far as the eye could see, he was alone. Nothing moved.

The wind was behind him though, and he could smell them. Wolves. There were wolves on his trail. He had to keep moving, outrun them, lead them far away from his herd. He stumbled and nearly fell but continued on.

Suddenly a hawk swooped down ahead of him and morphed into a human woman. She stood with her fists on her hips, waiting for him. "Derek Wheeler, you stop right there. Are you trying to kill yourself? Stop and rest. I won't let the wolves hurt you."

He tried to go around her, but she was quick. She caught hold of his mane and leaped onto his back. With a scream of challenge, he bucked her off, but she transformed to the hawk in midair and flew higher. A moment later she was back on the ground in human form again, still in front of him.

"Come on, Derek, stop screwing around. Stop running and rest."

There was something about her, something about her words, that began to penetrate his panicked mind. "Easy, Derek, slow down now, catch your breath." She was reaching for him now, moving beside him as he walked, for he could no longer run. "Easy, big fella, catch your breath."

That voice. It soothed him, called to him. He stopped walking and stood trembling as she caressed his neck. "Easy now, my brother, easy." She pulled up a handful of dry grass and began to rub him down. As he stood still the trembling became worse, he sank slowly to the ground and transformed into the man.

Derek Wheeler lay in the sun, gasping for air. She sat beside him, waiting for his breathing to calm down. "Feeling better?"

"Some, I guess."

"You're lucky you're immortal, a normal horse would be dead by now. I saw a water hole over that way. Once you're feeling up to it we'll talk a walk, get some water into you."

"Sounds good. What the hell happened?"

"What do you remember. Take your time, let it come back."

"I remember being a man, and then a horse. I remember you found me, then we met the wolves, your people. Jill came, then we were attacked by something, rustlers. Wolves, and something else, mad crazy, dangerous, killing. I guess I freaked out."

"The horse's response, Derek. There was gunfire, wolves, and the vampire, you panicked and ran. I'm just glad I found you in time."

"In time?"

"You were about done, my brother. Much farther and you'd have died on your feet."

"Yeah?"

"I'm a veterinarian, remember? I've seen a horse run to death before, and you were getting close."

"The wolves, I could smell the wolves getting closer, tried to lead them away from the herd, I ..."

"Easy now, brother, take it easy. You're seriously overheated. Just rest until the boys get here."

"But the wolves, I can smell them."

"I know. Think now, Derek, remember."

He sighed deeply and laid back on the grass. "Right, they're your wolves. Friends."

"That's right, my husband and his pack mate, our friends and protectors. When they get here, they'll help us get you to the water. Look, here they come now. Don't be afraid, they won't hurt you."

She stood and waved her arms. The two wolves trotted over to join them, transforming as they reached their resting place. "How's he doing?" asked Igor, as he hugged the woman and kissed her cheek.

"Derek's in bad shape, Igor, my love. He needs water and rest."

"Da, so do we all. There is water nearby, can he reach it?"

"Not without help."

He nodded then signaled Branimir. They each took an arm and raised Derek to his feet, then with his arms across their shoulders, he was practically carried to the water hole. They found a pack of coyotes already there. The coyotes turned as though to fight the weakened humans, but the wolves transformed again.

One look at those giant wolves decided the issue and the coyotes withdrew from the precious water hole. The two wolves stood guard while Derek drank his fill. "How's he doing, my pretty bird?"

"He's going to make it, sweetie. He'll need rest and lots of it, but he'll make it. The day's getting late, we should stay here tonight, and depending on how Derek's doing in the morning, maybe another day as well before we head back."

"Will he need medicine, Ronni?"

"No, rest and water, then food. He'll be fine. We'll take our time on the way back, so he can eat his fill along the way."

"So he travels as horse?"

"We'll all die of sunburn if we try to travel in human form, and you know it."

"Da, but I don't like it. If anyone sees us, a horse traveling with two wolves and a hawk will surely raise suspicions."

"You're right there, my love," sighed Rhonda. "All right, what's the alternative? Do I leave you guys here with him, so Derek can rest up for a few days while I go back for our people and bring help?"

"That was my thought on it," replied Igor.

"There's only one problem with that," she said.

"Me," said Derek. "You're afraid that if I go horse again, which we all know I will, will I still be here when you get back?"

"Yeah, that's about the sum of it, all right," said Rhonda. "Can you do it, brother Derek? Can you go horse, and still stay with the guys when they go wolf? Can you override the horse's instinct to run from the wolves?"

"I'll try my best."

"Not good enough," said Bran, "not by half. Look at this woman, she's the Lady Hawk. Even in flight she still thinks like the woman. Even as she finds our enemies, our prey, seeks out our friends while in the air as the hawk, she is still Ronni, still thinks like the woman. Hawk or woman, she thinks the same, why, because she knows who she is, no matter what form she's taken, she knows who she is.

"There's Igor, wolf, man, pack alpha, and yet, no matter what form he takes, still Igor, always Igor. The same for me. So, I ask you, Derek Wheeler, who are you? Do you know who you are?"

"I'd like to think so."

"Not good enough, not if you want to gain full control of the change. You can't be both, my friend, you can't. If you try, one day the horse will put the man in danger he cannot escape. If you try to be just the man one day the horse will gain control when it shouldn't, and you will die. Imagine driving on the highway at great speed then suddenly becoming the horse."

"Okay, I get it. So, help me here, how do I do this?"

Branimir grinned and lightly squeezed Derek's shoulder. "I will, first thing tomorrow we'll start the lessons to control the change.

Tonight, we sleep. I'm exhausted, that damn horse made me run all day without rest." They all chuckled at that.

Igor rose to his feet. "All right, people, get some sleep."

"Sweetheart?"

"Sweet Ronni, everybody is tired. Sleep now and I'll watch. Tomorrow you fly for help, Bran and Derek will practice, and Igor will sleep." He transformed into the wolf and settled down to watch.

Rhonda gave Branimir a look and he winked at her then closed his eyes. She nodded, then snuggled down beside Igor and went to sleep.

Next morning Rhonda was awake before the sun rose. She patted Igor's shoulder. "Go on now, my big bad wolf, go hunt. You need to eat." The stallion whickered softly, and she rose to her feet beside him as the wolf trotted off.

"Easy now, my brother, easy. You're safe here, the wolf won't hurt you. He does need to eat, though. You can survive on grass, but the wolf needs meat. I'll stay here with you while ..."

She was interrupted by a cry of fear and pain then silence. The horse snorted and tossed his head fearfully, but he stayed beside her. "Easy now, easy, big fella. Bran, that way." She pointed, and the second wolf trotted away. "Hush now, Brother Derek, easy now. The boys will soon be back."

Rhonda continued to sooth the big horse until the wolves returned. The horse danced cautiously away from Igor; the scent of blood was strong on him. Without a pause both wolves transformed and dove into the water hole. They rubbed themselves clean then came out. "Better?" asked Igor.

The horse stood still then shimmered into the man. "Jesus," he sighed as he rubbed his face with his hands. "I think I've got it."

"Got what? The change?" asked Rhonda.

"No, the fear. When I first became the horse, that stallion would never have run from two wolves, he'd have fought them to give the herd time to escape. He was fearless."

"What happened? Why did you run so far, so fast?" asked Igor.

"It was the other one, the woman, whatever the hell she was, or became. It caused a complete breakdown, utter blind fear. I remember. I started away, but turned back. Then I saw her, it, whatever it was, killing, so fast, so vicious, terrible ..."

"Easy, brother, easy now," soothed Rhonda as she put her arms around him. "Easy. That was Marlene. She's a vampire, but she's also one of us, a friend, family. Marlene will never hurt you."

He shuddered as he gained control of himself. "Yeah, I know. I know. I'm okay now. This fella is going to teach me control of the change. You go on, get help."

"And pants," chuckled Igor. She laughed, kissed his cheek, then leaped skyward, her piercing cry echoing across the plains as she disappeared in the distance.

They watched her go for a while until they could no longer see her. "Igor, you're a lucky man," sighed Derek, as he settled down on the ground.

"Da, I know, and give thanks every day."

"Can you tell me why she keeps calling me brother?"

"You've been adopted," replied Igor. "Derek, you're the same as my sweet Ronni, immortal. As time passes and I grow old you will see the dark truth of this. When I pass from this world into the great forest, she will be left behind, as will you. She will need you to comfort her."

"Jesus," breathed Derek. "Jill ..."

"Yes, your Jill the same. I will live longer than she, but it's the same. You will need Sweet Ronni when that day comes. She'll be there for you, and you must be there for her when her turn comes."

"You seem pretty pragmatic about it."

"What other option do I have, Derek? Should I ask the king to make me vampire? I would last only a few days before the Great Mother would be forced to kill me. The vampire lives every moment with the killing lust near the surface. Very few have ever learned to control it, those who can't are killed.

"For the wolf it's also an issue. If you add the vampire's needs to those of the wolf, there is no hope it could be controlled. No, I will live my life, enjoy each moment I have with my wild Lady Hawk, then I'll leave her behind as I pass into the mystery. She does her best to make every moment we have special, memorable, for she's well aware of the fate that awaits us.

"You must do the same for your Jill. Give her as much joy and love as you can, while you can, cherish her for what time you have. For this reason, if no other, you must gain control of the change. Break that horse to the saddle, control him, even as we do the wolf within."

"My god, Igor, how do you guys do it?"

"Just as we control the change, we push aside the awareness of what comes. It isn't here today, today we enjoy each other, and celebrate the life we have. That's the secret, my friend, live for today, for today is all we have."

Derek sat gazing at the water in the pool, lightly ruffled by the breeze. "She said there are others, like us."

"A few. There are nine vampires that we know of, one were-bear, one were-hawk, one were-mouse, and now the horse. In the end, as time passes without you, each other will be all you have. Come with us, get to know Torvil the bear, the king, and the rest. Bring your Jill with you, she will be welcomed."

He sat staring at the water for a while longer then Branimir reached over to grip his arm. "Listen, brother, you said that stallion was fearless. Show me that courage now, take control here, do what you must. No, you didn't ask for this, but it's come to you. Suck it up and deal with it."

Derek looked up and Branimir was grinning at him. "You're immortal, for fuck sake. Even if it kills you, you'll just revive to try again. What have you got to lose?"

Derek chuckled and shook his head. "Yeah, I guess you're right. There's not a damn thing I can do about any of it. Might as well start learning to cope. Okay, coach, what's the first step?"

Bran grinned and slapped his shoulder. "Turn horse, eat grass, drink water, but remember the man. While you do these things, in your mind, remember Jill's birthday, your anniversary, your mother's birthday, your own, your first bicycle. Feed and nourish the horse but think human thoughts while you do.

"When you're ready, return to us. We'll be in wolf form. Have no fear of us, for we're your herd now, and you're one of our pack. Okay?"

"Got it," said Derek, as he rose to his feet. A moment later he shimmered into the stallion and began to graze.

THE SUN WAS JUST SETTING as the hawk spiraled down and morphed into the woman right beside Merle as he walked from the barn to the house. "Jesus woman," he exclaimed.

"Hey, Merle."

"Girl, you look like hell."

"Really? I'm standing here, buck naked, and you say I look like shit? I'm hurt, Merle."

"What? No, tired, I mean tired. You look exhausted."

"Nice recovery, Slick."

She was grinning, and he blushed to his roots. "You're as bad as the rest of them. Git in that house and get some clothes on. Git."

With a laugh of pure mischief, she danced up the steps and into the house. A grinning Marlene handed her a robe and a bottle of water. Rhonda thanked her, swept the robe about her shoulders, and then drained the bottle. "Where is everybody?"

"Elaine was getting twitchy, so I sent her back with Amanda in the plane. We figure we'll have to take Derek back in a horse trailer."

"Good call."

"Igor can bust my chops for taking over without consulting him first, but she needed to go."

"Marlene, you're like his big sister. You can get away with anything with Igor, he'll never say a word, and you know it. Besides, it was the right call and he'll agree.

"So, here's where we stand. Derek's with the boys, and he's promised to stay there until I get back but, that horse is afraid of the wolves and deathly afraid of the vampire."

"Me?"

"You. It was you at full vamp that panicked him. Damn near killed himself before I could get him stopped. He's okay, and resting, but we need to get there as soon as we can."

"What do we need to do?" asked Jill.

"Bring extra food and clothes, as well as horses for Igor and Bran. If anyone sees a horse running with two dire wolves, well, you get the idea. Get the map and I'll show you where they are. I'll fly back tomorrow and hold them at that water hole. Once you get there, we'll start back as a group of humans with an extra horse."

"If he's skittish around Marlene," said Larise, "perhaps she and I should stay back and see if we can run interference about the dead rustlers. That's going to be a holy mess to cover up."

"Good plan, sis," sighed Rhonda. "I like it. Now, as Merle so delicately observed, I'm beat to a rag and need ten hours of sleep."

"First, I feed you, girl," said Peggy. "You're too skinny. All that flying around without food isn't healthy."

"Thanks, Peggy, I appreciate that. You're right, I know. Heck, Merle hardly gave me a second look when I got here."

Merle chuckled and shook his head. "Stop it woman, you're killing me."

"Sorry, Merle."

"The hell you are."

"The funny thing is, before I was changed I wouldn't be caught dead letting anyone see me naked. Now I'm hardly even aware of it. I shift back and forth between the woman and the hawk so fast and often, it's hard to remember to have somebody bring a robe or something. The nudity just feels natural now."

"Ah-huh," said Merle, as Rhonda finished the meal Peggy had given her.

"Okay, Merle, you got me, I'm actually a wanton exhibitionist, and ..."

"All right, that's enough, off to bed with you, young lady," grinned Peggy. "Right this way."

Peggy showed her to a room, but as she started away, Rhonda reached for her arm. "Peggy, I'm sorry. You have to know ..."

"Easy, girl. I saw how you look at that young fella. Besides, with you running around naked all the time, old Merle has started to remember what it's like to be frisky. Girl, I can see how it is for you. I'm okay here, we're okay."

"Thank you," replied Rhonda, as she hugged the woman and kissed her cheek.

"Go on now, into bed with you," smiled Peggy, as she returned the hug then stepped away and closed the door.

Heading Back

The next morning they rode out, Jill, Peggy, and Merle. They took a pack horse with extra clothing and food for the boys, as well as saddle horses for them. Rhonda flew on ahead. It was late in the day when she arrived, but there was no one there. She landed and looked all around but saw nothing.

Rhonda stomped her foot in frustration. "Dammit, where are they? Shit, I wish I could follow a scent like these guys. Come on, Ronni, think. Think girl, think, what could have happened?

"Okay, Derek could have taken off again. The boys would surely go after him. No, the three of them seemed to be good, and there was no vampire here, so they should have been all right.

"So, why would he run away? Something else frightened him. What? What could do that with two dire wolves to help protect him? So, no scared horse, what else? Could the stallion have taken him over again and gone looking for his herd? Maybe, but I doubt that.

"Come on, Ronni, think. Where would they go, and why? Dammit, I need Igor's nose here, I need a scent to follow. Wait, I'm eyes, not nose, but where to look? The ground, look at the ground. Humans used to be trackers.

"Okay, the ground is soft beside the water. There, we have horse tracks, wolf tracks, wait, that's a horseshoe track. Derek's a wild horse, so no shoes on Derek. Crap, that's a boot track. So, men on horses. Men on horses carry guns so my guys take off, but which way?

"Think, Ronni. What would Igor do? Ah, my big bad wolf wouldn't go that far unless he had to. He'd find cover. Okay, then the men hunt him, but Igor would hunt the men too. It's open here, far too open for this game. Men with rifles have all the advantages. So, Igor would look for trees, jumbled rocks, hills, anything to shorten the sight lines for the men.

"So, now I know what to look for."

With that she leaped into the air and transformed, climbing high. Slowly the hawk made a wide circle. From the ground she was only a speck on the fading daylight, but nothing on the ground escaped her notice.

There, in the distance, a line of trees. She arrowed towards that line to see a stream flowing slowly through a dense copse of cottonwood trees. The flicker of a campfire showed two men sitting beside it. A moment later the movement caught her eye, two hunting wolves moving through the trees.

The two men continued to talk, unaware that death stalked them on silent paws. The hawk widened her circle, the wolves could handle the hunters, she needed to find the stallion. There, beside the stream, a shadow amid the gathering shadows, a silent part of the forest around him.

She came in low and perched on a branch where he could see her. Once she had his attention she dropped to the ground, shimmering into the woman as she fell, to land lightly on her feet. The horse transformed into the man.

She laid her finger along her lips for silence as she approached him. "So, you found us, Igor said you'd work it out and come."

"Are you okay, brother Derek?"

"I'm good, my sister."

Rhonda gently gripped his arm as she gazed into his eyes. "Igor explained it to you, did he?"

"Took a while to get it through my head, but, yeah, he did. Jesus, Ronni, how do you do it? How ..."

She put her finger to his lips. "One day at a time, brother," she said, "just one day at a time, and suck every minute of joy out of it I can. Jill will catch up with us tomorrow, and you can't be all gooey-eyed when she does. Love her as hard as you can for as long as you can."

He drew a deep breath and nodded. "Okay, I will. I'm starting to get it."

She smiled and stepped back. "Stay here, I'm going to go check on the guys."

"I can help."

"Look, I don't want to be chasing you halfway to Canada. You know what the wolves are going to do."

"Is the vampire with them?"

He was grinning and so was she. "Nope."

"Then I'm good."

"All right, you move closer, quiet as you can, but don't get into the action until you hear the cry of the hawk." He nodded then morphed into the stallion. She leaped into the air and silently rose out of sight.

Back at the men's campsite, they'd gone on alert. One man was on his feet, a rifle in his hands. "Relax, man, there's nothing out there."

"Thought I heard something. You didn't get a clear shot at that wolf; he could still be alive. That was one damn big wolf. I wouldn't want him to find me asleep in the blanket."

"Scared of the big bad wolf? Hey, want me to tell you a bedtime story?"

"Oh, shut the hell up."

Overhead, the hawk saw the men, and the wolves moving in through the shadows. She didn't want that rifle used on her men. She swooped down to transform into the woman a short way from the humans, yet neither had seen her. "Hey there, fellas, mind if I warm up beside that fire?"

Both men turned to stare at the beautiful naked woman who approached them. As the rifle slipped from his hands, the slack-jawed man didn't see the wolf charging. It knocked him flying, the rifle falling at Rhonda's feet. The second man sat with wide frightened eyes staring at the gigantic wolf that stood over him.

At the woman's whistle, the wolves backed away slightly. She raised the rifle and aimed it loosely at the man who'd dropped it. "Okay, fellas, listen up now, we're going to relieve you of a few things, starting with your britches. Get 'em off, now."

Neither man moved, so she spoke again. "Do it. Get your clothes off or I'll set the boys on you." Both wolves snarled and moved closer. The terrified men suddenly came to life and began to shuck off their clothes. "Much better. Now, we're going to keep your stuff, clothes, guns, horses, money, all of it. You get to keep your lives as long as you do as your told."

"What do you want?"

"I want you to head for town now and don't look back. When the sheriff asks you what happened, tell him you were robbed by Lady Godiva." She gave the cry of the hawk and the big red stallion trotted out to her. She grabbed his mane and swung up onto his back. "Get moving."

"Naked? You'd make us walk three days barefoot and buck-assed naked?"

She wrenched a shell into the firing chamber and leveled the rifle at him. "I could just shoot you then feed your carcass to the wolves. Your choice, boys, but decide now 'cause I'm starting to get cranky."

Both men turned and quickly headed away from their camp, bitching and yelping as tender feet touched a rock. Rhonda followed on the horse. Darkness had fully fallen, and they couldn't see their fire when they finally noticed the woman was no longer behind them.

Back at the campsite, Rhonda was cuddled into Igor's arms. Bran was in wolf form, watching. "Lady Godiva?" Derek raised as eyebrow as he spoke. She laughed.

"Think about it," grinned Igor. "They'll be found, tell their story, then get thrown in the drunk tank for a while."

"Yeah, pretty cool idea at that, sister."

"What happened, guys? They catch you napping?"

"There were five of them at first," said Igor. "They came riding in hard, shouting, waving ropes in the air, and shooting guns. We ran. They tried to turn us away, but Derek's horse knew of this place. He poured on the speed and led us to the trees. Once in the trees, we hid from them, not so hard to do in there.

"Anyway, one got a shot at Bran and hit him, but not bad. We hid and rested, planning to kill them tonight. I like your solution better." He kissed the top of her head and smiled. "We heard them talking. Three of them went back for a truck to haul away the horses they'd captured. They tried to get Derek too, but he's too fast and smart."

"Okay, if they went for a truck, there must be a road near here. I'll go up and take a look in the morning.

"Jill, Peggy, and Merle are on their way to that water hole with food and clothes for you guys. Derek, what do you think, can you hold human form long enough to ride back with us?"

"That's still a work in progress, sis. We're probably better off if I travel in horse mode."

"Yeah? How are the lessons coming?"

Derek grinned. "Coach Bran says I'm getting the hardest part under control."

"The hardest part?"

"Holding my thoughts human while in horse form. He says that's the key."

She smiled. "He's right there. I rode shotgun for the hawk for months before I managed to get that part under control. The animal is so fierce and strong. It knows exactly what it wants, what it needs to do, and has no impulse control. By the time your human mind starts to reason something out, the animal has already acted."

"Yep, that's about right," he sighed, "but I'm getting a handle on it. Keeping my thoughts on Jill is working for me."

Rhonda smiled and patted his arm as she snuggled deeper into Igor's embrace. "That'll do it. Okay, so you travel in animal form. Igor and Bran can run as wolf until we meet up with the troops, then they can ride back."

Just then Bran reappeared from the darkness. "Those two whiners are about a mile that way, hiding behind rocks. They're even too embarrassed to lie together for shared body heat."

Rhonda waved him closer. "Let me see that wound, now." He sat beside her, and she began to inspect the injury. "You got lucky there, Bran. An inch or two lower and you'd have a shattered shoulder joint. As is, I can fix that right up for you if those morons had a first aid kit with them."

She rose and began rummaging through their saddlebags, eventually finding what she was looking for. A few minutes and a couple of groans from Bran later he was all bandaged up. "Stop whining," she grinned. "Larise would skin me alive if I let her boy get hurt."

"Lady Hawk, you have no idea how weird that sounds coming from you."

"I know, Bran, but since the king marked her, I've grown to like the girl."

"Da, me too."

"Good thing, since you married her."

"You think?"

She laughed at that. "Yeah, I do. Okay, I'm beat, one of you guys can watch. I need to sleep."

"Okay, you guys rest, I'll watch." So saying, Derek rose and put out the fire, then transformed into the stallion. Igor and Bran went wolf and snuggled Rhonda between them. She was smiling as she drifted off to sleep.

ABOUT NOON THE NEXT day, the group of riders came upon two naked men, limping along under the hot sun. The men called out and asked them for help. "What the merry hell are you two idiots doing out here, buck naked?" asked Merle, as he leaned his arms on the pommel of his saddle.

"We were robbed," said one of the men.

"Robbed, is that your story?" Peggy was grinning, and the embarrassed men tried to hide their genitals behind their hands.

"Yes, we were. Come on, you gotta have something in them saddle bags, blankets or something."

"You know what I think," said Jill. "I think you two jackasses were stealing horses, and somebody caught you. I'm thinking we should just go about our business and pretend we never saw you."

"Come on, you can't just leave us here. Give us a blanket and a loan of a horse to get us into town. We need to let the sheriff know about that bitch."

"Which bitch would that be?" asked Peggy.

"Said her name was Lady Godiva ..."

"Shut up, Greg, Jesus."

"Lady Godiva?" said Merle. "A skinny girl, right pretty, runs around naked, probably riding a big red horse, right?"

"Yeah, that's right. You know that bitch?"

"Never heard of her," grinned Merle, as he urged his horse onward. The two men were still swearing as the riders disappeared over a hill.

A short while later a hawk spiraled down from the sky, glided past Merle, then flew off in a new direction. "You don't suppose that was her?"

"Yeah, Merle," grinned Peggy, "I bet that was the little girl, all right."

"But she went off in the wrong direction."

"Something must have happened," said Jill, as she urged her horse in the direction taken by the hawk. Three hours later they found them. The hawk gave a piercing cry from overhead then spiraled down to transform into the woman. She waved them over.

As they approached, Igor shimmered from the wolf into the man. "Hey there, young fella," called Peggy, a twinkle in her eye.

"Hi, did you have any trouble finding us?"

"Not a bit," she replied, her grin widening.

She winked at Rhonda who gave a hearty laugh. "Igor, put some pants on. You too, Bran."

Jill tossed a bundle of clothes to each of them, and they hastily dressed. "So, you planning to ride back too?" she asked, as Rhonda pulled on her boots and jeans then settled a t-shirt over her head.

"Yep."

"But we didn't bring a horse for you."

"That's okay, I'll ride yours."

"Mine?"

"Yeah, I thought you'd want to ride that one," she grinned, as Derek came racing over the hill.

He skidded to a stop right beside them and morphed into the man. "We've got incoming." He was instantly back in horse form again, nuzzling at Jill. She laughed with delight and hopped down from the saddle. She grabbed a handful of his mane then leaped to his back.

Rhonda was instantly in the saddle Jill had vacated, Igor and Bran were mounted as well. A group of men came over the hill and approached. "Afternoon, folks."

"Afternoon," replied Merle.

"Did you happen to see two men around here anywhere?"

"Yep," replied Merle. "They were back that way a few miles. Both stark naked and talking crazy. Didn't want that sort of thing around the women, so we rode away."

"So, what are you doing way out here?"

"Minding my own damn business," replied Merle. "Now, I don't really care what sort of drugs you're importing or making, but if I was you, I wouldn't be letting the hired hands play with it, you know?

"Now, as I recall, there's a water hole nearby where we can camp for the night, then we'll be on our way."

"Yeah, about that ..."

"Don't do it friend," said Igor, as he leveled a gun at the man's head. "Just move your hands away from that rifle slowly, nobody needs to die today. You've got your business to attend to, and we have ours. Go find your two friends and we'll continue on our way."

The man swallowed hard and moved his hand away from his gun. Merle pointed the direction. "That way, about two or three miles. You can't miss 'em." The riders turned and followed their leader away.

"I don't trust those guys," said Igor.

"Nor do I," agreed Merle. "I know another way back to the ranch. They think we're headed for the water hole, but we'll be a long way from there by dark. Let's go."

They crossed the ridge, then down and a circle to the right, along a narrow gully, then out onto the plains again. As darkness fell, Igor cautioned against a fire. "Fire at night can be seen for a long way, best to remain in darkness."

"Da, everybody sleep, I'll watch," said Branimir, as he shimmered into the wolf. "Good plan," agreed Igor. "Merle, can we reach the ranch by tomorrow?"

"Be late, but if we push we could make it."

"Then we'll push. I'm getting a bad feeling about this."

Mystery Solved

While the riders pushed for home base, Larise and Marlene tracked down the sheriff. He was organizing a search party when a car came up the dirt road and the two women got out. "Agent Parker, that you?"

"In the flesh, Sheriff. What's going on?"

"These two trucks were found by a couple of kids out racing their dirt bikes along this road. Looked like rustlers, so I came out to have a look. About the same time somebody reported several men missing. I gathered a few people and came out to have a look.

"So why are you here?"

"Looking for Bill and Mona Higgins. They own the place near where Mr. Wheeler disappeared. I want to ask them a few questions."

"Well you're in luck, they're right here. Bill!"

A nervous man and woman came to where the sheriff was talking to two official looking women. "What's up, Sheriff?"

"Bill, this is Agent Parker of the FBI, she wants to ask you a few questions."

"Questions? About what?"

"Mr. Higgins, do you own a 30-06 Springfield hunting rifle?"

"Well, yeah, so?"

"Do you have it with you?"

"What's this all about?"

"I have reason to believe you may be involved in the disappearance and possible murder of Derek Wheeler. He was on the property next to yours when he disappeared."

"Murder? I didn't murder anybody."

"A spent casing from a 30-06 was found in the rocks near where Mr. Wheeler disappeared."

"No way, I took that ... Oh shit." He began to back away, but the sheriff stopped him. Terrified, he looked from the sheriff to Larise and back again. "Look, I didn't kill nobody. I just shot that rock beside that fool. I expected the horse to kick the shit out of him. The damn rock exploded, and when the dust settled, they were both gone. I didn't kill nobody."

"Mr. Higgins, I have it on good authority that you've been known to associate with suspected rustlers. Tell me, are we going to find anything interesting around here?"

Bill Higgins shrank away from Larise, but Mona stepped forward to defend him. "Look, I was there when he shot the rock. If Bill'd shot at Wheeler, his body would have still been there, same for out there."

"Excuse me?" asked the Sheriff.

"Bill, for god's sake, tell him. I'd rather face a rustling charge than a murder charge."

The fight went out of Bill then. "All right, we were here, but we stayed back to watch the trucks. The rest rode out to gather horses. It took a long while, and it was dark when most of them came back."

"Most?"

"Yeah, Sheriff, two guys were still out there. The others were hoping they had more success. A while later, one of the guys thought he saw someone sneaking around the camp, so they rode out again. It didn't take long before we heard the gunfire, then nothing.

"By daybreak they weren't back, so I rode out to have a look. They were all dead when I found them, looked like they'd been torn apart by wolves or bears. Jesus. I came back, then me and Mona beat it for home. Scared the shit outta me when you showed up this morning."

"Well now, it looks like you can save this search party a lot of time. How about you show us where those bodies are."

"All right, Sheriff. They're out that way."

"You can wait here if you want to, Agent Parker. I promise I'll bring him back."

She grinned and nodded as the search party set out. It was a couple of hours before they returned. Bill Higgins was in restraints when they arrived. The sheriff dismounted and sighed as he brushed the dust from his jeans.

"Well, Agent Parker, you and I have a small problem."

"Oh?" Larise stepped in front of Marlene who had just gotten a defensive look. "How's that, Sheriff?"

"It seems we both have dibs on the same prisoner."

"Bill Higgins? He's all yours, Sheriff. He claims he didn't shoot Mr. Wheeler, there was no body and no blood at the scene, so I have no real reason to arrest him. May I assume you do?"

"Oh, hell yes. I've got five dead bodies out there. The damn coyotes have made a mess of them, but he confessed to being part of the rustling gang, and he knew exactly where to find the bodies, he knew they were there and didn't report it. Yeah, I've got plenty of reason to hold him."

"He's all yours, Sheriff. I'm willing to accept his story about not shooting Mr. Wheeler. I'm sort of going with my first hunch on that one."

"You think Bill helped Wheeler?"

"I've seen his ranch. Pretty sure he could be had for a few hundred, if you know what I mean."

The sheriff chuckled at that. "Yep, that wouldn't surprise me at all."

"All right, Sheriff, I guess we'll get out of your way and let you work. Let's get out of this heat, Marlene."

They climbed into their car and slowly drove away. "Oh, thank God for air conditioning," sighed Marlene, as she switched it up on bust. Larise chuckled as she turned onto the paved highway.

They rode in silence for a while then Marlene spoke again. "Larise?"

"Your instincts screaming too?"

"Yes indeed. Something's not quite right here. I had the sense that the sheriff had more on his mind, but wasn't ready to talk yet."

"Yeah, he was hiding something all right. I'll bet he ran my badge number and found out it was expired. Terry promised to get me a new up-to-date one, but they were called to New York before he could follow through."

"So, what do you want to do here?"

"Actually, I'm hoping Igor will get back and we can get on the road before it all goes to hell on us."

"When was it ever that easy?"

"Sadly, Marlene, my friend, I can't think of a single time. I believe it's time to shift gears here."

"You mean go back to the ranch and start packing?"

"Yeah, that, and maybe head off trouble before it starts. You may end up using the compulsion quite a bit before this is over."

"I was thinking the same thing."

WHILE IGOR AND CREW hurried back toward the ranch, Elaine was getting distracted at the castle. "Elaine? Elaine, honey, are you okay? That's the second time I've spoken to you."

Suddenly embarrassed and frightened, the girl apologized to the queen. "Oh my god, Queen Sally, I'm so sorry. Please, it won't happen again. I ..."

"Stop this now and give me your hands."

"What???"

"You're upset, and it's about your sister, but you can't get a clear read. We'll do it together. Give me your hands." Elaine swallowed hard, then sat and extended her hands to the queen. "Now, deep breaths," said the queen, as she took Elaine's hands in her own. "That's it, deep breaths, now release yourself to the vision."

A few moments later their eyes popped open at the same time. Sally rose to her feet, still holding Elaine's hand. "Come, we need to speak to the king." They hurried away together in search of King Harald.

They found him in the exercise room, but he wasn't practicing with the sword, he was staring out the window, brooding. He turned to face them as they hurried to his side. "Sally, what is it? Is it about Igor and the others?"

"Yes. How did you know?"

"Larise is troubled, I can feel it. That girl can usually handle whatever is thrown at her, so her trepidation disturbs me. What have my two favorite psychics seen?"

"There's trouble, Harald," sighed the queen as she sat beside him. "I get the sense that Derek is at the heart of it. I also sense that there is far more danger to us all from this than we might realize."

"How do you mean?"

"Honey, I believe Igor and the others can handle whatever comes at them. What I fear comes after that. Something has already happened that has turned prying eyes in our direction."

"Prying eyes? The government? Has Egan Bridger betrayed us?"

"No, love, this is at a much lower level than Mr. Bridger, but all raging rivers begin with a trickle of water somewhere. We need to find out where that trickle is and divert it long before it brings close scrutiny in our direction."

"Can you get a clear picture of where that might be?"

"No, but I believe it to be in Igor's field of operation. I believe we should warn him."

The king nodded and pulled out his phone. Eventually he gave up and sighed as he gazed out the window. "I can't reach him or Rhonda. I was hoping I wouldn't have to do this, but I guess I'll have to call Larise or Marlene."

"You don't want to undermine Igor's authority?"

"Or his sense of my faith in him. He's still young, I don't want to undermine his self-confidence, especially not now. Ah well, there's no help for it." Just then his phone buzzed, and he grinned as he glanced at it. "Larise?"

"You wanted to talk to me, Sire?"

"Indeed, I do. Larise, something, or somebody, out where you are is getting far too nosy about certain things."

"That would be the local sheriff, Sire."

"Perhaps, but Sally says he's not the main concern. His curiosity has set others in motion."

"Sire, if the internal system has taken an interest, there's only one way to stop it now. Terry will have to call in a few favors from Director Bridger, the sooner the better."

"I'll set that in motion, now tell me what else has gone sideways out there."

"Well, it actually hasn't happened yet, but I've got a bad feeling."

"As do I. Larise, I can't locate Igor or Rhonda, do you know where they are and what's happened?"

"Yes, Sire. Derek panicked and bolted. According to Lady Hawk he ran halfway to Canada before they got him stopped. Igor and Bran have gone wolf to find him and bring him back. We're hoping to see them arrive tomorrow. I'll tell him to report in as soon as he gets here, but he's well out on the plains right now."

"Fair enough. You do what you can, and I'll see if I can reach Terry."

King Harald dropped the phone back into his pocket then noticed the faces of the two women. "What, there's more?"

"Harald, when Elaine and I join hands and focus, we're far stronger. We both saw that empty house on our second farm being occupied by Elaine's friends, Peggy and Merle. We also saw several horses grazing in those empty fields attached to that farm. You did say Bill could use the help."

"So, the family's about to get bigger?"

"If they survive," sighed Elaine.

"They will, Elaine," said Sally, patting the girl's hand. "Yes, there'll be danger, but we didn't see any death, did we?"

"It's all so frightening."

"Yes, but we'll have to trust Igor and his team to handle this, get them here unharmed. Come on, you and I'll go take a closer look at that farmhouse."

"And I'll go set Tommy to work on obliterating any attempts to infiltrate us electronically, then I'll call Terry, and then ..." He chuckled as he realized he was talking to himself; the two women had already left the room. He scooped up his shirt then followed them out.

Later that night he cuddled his queen in his arms. "Sally?"

"It's starting to unravel, Harald. We're getting close to the tipping point."

"But we're not there yet, there's still time to head this off, yes?"

"There is, but still, I'm frightened."

Horse Thieves

The sheriff and his deputy stood watching Larise drive away. "So, you're just going to let her drive away?"

"Yep, I've got no real reason to hold her just yet, but she did confirm my suspicions."

"Oh?"

"Yeah, she waited here to make sure we found the bodies, but she gave up old Bill pretty easy."

"So, you think she's in on all the horse thieving that's been going on around here lately?"

The sheriff swept off his hat and wiped away the sweat from his brow with his sleeve. "I truly do. Think about it, horse rustling suddenly goes way up, we start getting an idea of what's going on then, bam, Wheeler disappears, and his woman makes a fuss to distract us.

"We just put that on the back burner and Parker shows up, uses an old badge to claim the Wheeler file, further muddying the waters. Now dead bodies start showing up and she throws Bill under the bus. Once again, she knocked us off track."

"What tipped you off to her, Sheriff?"

"The whole damned thing seemed fishy to me. My brother-in-law works for the FBI as a computer geek. I asked him to check her out, and he says that she disappeared from their records two years ago. Some dark and fancy government spy agency scooped her up. Last fall she dropped off their radar, then showed up here. Why? What the hell is really going on here?"

"Wow, Boss, your brother-in-law must have some super clearance to get all that."

"Naw, between you and me, he's probably the best hacker in the business."

"He hacked the FBI?"

"And a few others."

"Jesus, Sheriff. I sure hope you have a plan, because if she's a spook, they could come after you."

"Yeah, well, that's the plan. I'm going to haul her ass in on rustling charges and see who shows up, what bullshit story they tell."

"Sheriff, you're playing with fire here. I just hope I don't get burned along with you."

"Relax, I've got friends in the media watching the whole thing. Come on, let's get these prisoners back to town and get out of the heat. I'm cooking out here."

KING HARALD SAT IN his favorite chair, brooding. Nearby, Tommy Dawson, the king's resident electronics genius, was swearing under his breath while he worked frantically. "Ha, got you there, you dirty sonofabitch. Oh no you don't, it's not that easy. Ha, saw that one coming too. Shit, oh man, that was close."

"Tommy?"

"Sorry, Sire, but we have a problem."

"Tell me."

"Somebody's started looking into Larise's past, as you suspected. He's good, too damn good. The more I try to redirect his attention the more determined he becomes to find us. He's almost here. I may have to do a power cut and blow everything to hell and back, but if I do they'll know where we are."

Herald was on the edge of his seat. "How much time have we got."

"Not a lot. I can fend him off for another half hour or so, but it's getting dicey."

"Do you know where this person is, in the flesh, I mean."

"Yes, sir. I just now managed to pull up his location. Sir, he's working from a computer in his home. I just sent his picture and address to your phone."

"Keep at it, Tommy. Shut him down if you can. What city is he in?"

"Riverton." The king walked out of the room, his phone to his ear.

MARLENE SIGHED AND dropped her phone back into her lap for a moment. "Slow down, Larise, we've got a problem." She picked up the phone again and began searching Google Maps. A moment later she had it. "Okay, here's the address. Get us there, all possible speed."

Larise entered the address into the GPS then set out. Driving as fast as she dared, she wove her way through the town and out into the suburbs. "Can you tell me what's up?"

"Yeah, the sheriff checked into your ID and found your badge number was no longer active."

"Oh shit."

"Yeah, and he must have a connection somewhere, because he's got a hacker tracking us down. Apparently, this hacker is really good, and Tommy can't hold him off for long."

"How much does this guy know?"

"Too much. Way the hell too much, and he's set off red flags in a number of government departments."

"I repeat, oh shit."

"Our job is to stop him, shut him down permanently. Poor Tommy will have to defuse and redirect the government interest. I expect Terry and Gudrun will be calling on Director Bridger as well."

"Fair enough. Here's our street, three houses from the next intersection, there, that's the place." Larise barely had the car stopped before Marlene was out and kicking in the front door of the house.

As they charged through the broken door a woman screamed. "What are you doing here? Who are you? What ..."

The tall balding man stopped talking as Larise's gun pointed at his chest. "Everyone freeze and nobody gets hurt." She flashed her badge. "Find him, Marlene, I've got this."

The vampire swept through the house and found two more people, but no computer hacker at work. "*Be silent. Go down stairs and join your family. Make no threatening moves and obey the woman with the gun.*"

The two women followed her as she raced down and headed for the basement. There she found a young man, bent over his computer, headphones on, and oblivious to the world around him. He screamed in terror as he was jerked from the chair and needle-sharp fangs bit deeply into his neck. He struggled for only a moment then went limp in her grasp.

Fighting the urge to drink him dry, she thrust him away and he sank toward the floor. As he did, his computer began to delete files. Everything vanished from the screen, then the vampire jerked it from the desk and smashed it on the floor.

"*Pay attention. You're afraid of computers, they're not safe, and you don't like them. You will refuse to ever touch one again. You will never speak of the research you've been doing for the sheriff. You will never speak a word about shapeshifters as long as you live. You have a deep desire to learn plumbing as a career choice.*

"*Rest now for an hour then clean this mess up and throw that computer into the garbage.*"

She left him there and returned to the main floor where Larise was holding the rest of the family at gunpoint. "*Everyone stand still.*" They all froze in place.

"All right, Larise, go start the car. I'll take care of this and be right out." Larise grinned and nodded as she turned and vanished through the broken door.

"Listen carefully. You were home all day. Nothing unusual happened. The young man in the basement is deathly afraid of computers, always has been. You have never seen me or my companion, you will not recognize us or pictures of us if they are shown to you.

"Some vandals broke your front door. You will count slowly to one hundred then set about repairing the damage. Begin." With that Marlene ran from the house and jumped into the car with Larise.

"We all clear?"

"We're clear. I'll call the king and report in." A moment later he was on the line. "Yes, Harald, we shut him down and destroyed his computer. I left him a command to forget computers and become a plumber."

"A plumber?"

"A fitting career for a man who likes stirring up shit, or so I thought."

The king chuckled at that. "Marlene de France, you're a bad woman. Well done."

"A plumber?" asked Larise, as she maneuvered a tight turn.

"Seemed like a good idea at the time," grinned Marlene.

Larise laughed at that. "Woman, you rock."

"Thank you, thank you. You can slow down now; we got there in time."

"We were lucky there, but I have a bad feeling. This isn't over yet, not by half."

"Okay, Agent Parker, I trust your instincts. What's our next move?"

"We get back to the ranch and pack up. As soon as they arrive, we load up and get on the road. At least, that's what I'd like to do, Igor may have other ideas."

Marlene sighed and relaxed back in her seat. "Only one way to find out. I say we go with your plan until he says different."

"Works for me."

Marlene and Larise arrived back at the ranch house to find it locked up. Marlene expertly picked the lock and they were inside. Once the packing up was done they loaded the bags into the SUV then headed for the barn.

Larise was astounded as Marlene picked up the end of the horse trailer and pulled it to the old truck Jill drove. She attached the hitch then noticed Larise grinning at her. "What?"

"You're as handy to have around as a bag of nails, you know that?"

Marlene laughed at that. "Shut up, Larise."

They returned to the house to raid the kitchen. With snacks in hand, they went back to the barn, guessing that, should any danger come, it would look for them in the house. They were right.

IGOR PUSHED THEM HARD, but nobody complained. Twice, Merle had reminded him to let the horses rest a bit, but each time they were soon on the go again. The ranch was nearly in sight when Igor called a halt. The horses stood breathing deeply, grateful for the rest.

"Igor, what is it?" asked Rhonda.

"I've got a bad feeling."

"Da, me too," muttered Branimir. "Something's not right. Should we take a look?"

"My job," sang Rhonda, then her horse shied away as the hawk exploded into the air from the saddle. Igor grumbled something about an impatient woman as he dismounted and gathered her clothes. The others dismounted as well, and the grateful horses began to graze while everyone waited for the Lady Hawk to return.

It was only a few minutes, but it seemed longer to Igor. He looked up at her call and watched as she dove towards the ground, leveled off to transform, completed a two and a half backward somersault, then land lightly on her feet. "And she sticks the landing," she exulted, as Igor tossed her clothes to her.

"Nicely done, my pretty bird. So, was there anything amiss at the ranch?"

"I couldn't see anything, but Larise's car is there, and the horse trailer's already hitched to the truck. I couldn't see the girls, so they're either in the house or the barn."

"You didn't go down to see?"

"No, sweetheart, something felt off and my hawk didn't want anything to do with getting closer. She senses trouble, even as you did. Anyway, as far as I can tell, it's clear at the moment."

"Then we need to get back there, get loaded up and on the road. The sooner we get some distance from this place the better I'll feel."

"Second that," agreed Branimir.

"Then we go," said Igor, as he swung easily into the saddle.

"I gotta give you credit, Igor," said Merle, as they rode down the hill. "For a man who says he's never ridden a horse before, you're sure looking comfortable in the saddle now."

"Then I've got you fooled. My ass is falling off and my bones hurt." That brought a few chuckles at his expense.

They were just nearing the corral when they saw the cars racing up the driveway, lights flashing and sirens blaring. "Ronni, go!" Once again the horse shied as the hawk exploded from its back. The rest rode toward the barn and the oncoming cars.

The sheriff's car skidded to a halt and two men leaped out, guns drawn. The other three cars did the same. "Freeze," the sheriff bawled over the bullhorn. "Hands in the air where I can see them."

They dismounted and put their hands in the air. "What's going on, Sheriff?" asked Igor as he took a step forward.

"I said freeze," shouted the sheriff. "Hands behind your head, down on the ground, now. I said get down."

Three men with drawn weapons charged at Igor, but he put his hands behind his neck and sank to his knees. He winked at Bran as he did. "My ID's in my pocket, Sheriff. You might want to take a look at it."

"I've seen all the fake ID from you lot that I want to see. Now where the hell is Parker, I know she's around here somewhere."

Merle took a step forward. "Sheriff, what the hell crawled up your ass and died? This man's a federal agent."

"The hell he is, he's a goddamn horse thief and so are you."

"What???"

"The jig's up, Merle. My brother-in-law got the goods on your fake federal agents. I know damn well you people are working with the horse rustlers. There's no sense denying it, we've got you for rustling and murder."

"Murder?"

"Yep, we got your truck with the herd of horses, plus a half dozen dead bodies, and two crazy horse thieves who turned evidence against you. Now, we're carting you all off to jail and that herd of horses is going for dog food. Nice of you to bring the stallion in for us, that makes the whole herd ..."

The sheriff got no further as the stallion exploded away, back toward the hills. As everyone looked, Igor moved. Before anyone could react, there were two men down and the sheriff was staring at the barrel of a gun that was touching his nose. "Drop the weapons or the sheriff dies with me."

Reluctantly, they started to lower their guns. As the guns hit the ground, Igor stripped the bull horn from the sheriff's hand and raised it to his lips. "Marlene, Larise, are you near?"

"Right here, Agent Wolf," sang Larise, as she and Marlene trotted from the barn.

Igor was studying the sky as they reached him. "Shit, she's gone after him again. This is starting to piss me off. It's taking far too long, and every time we start to get a handle on it he runs away and she goes after him. I promise you; this will be the last time."

"Easy, Igor, easy," soothed Marlene. "Let me deal with this, then we'll work through it."

"Are you going to kill Derek?" asked Jill, tears running down her face.

"Let me, Igor."

"Do it, Marlene."

"All law enforcement personnel drop your weapons and look at the sky." To a man they instantly obeyed. *"Good, now, there has been a mistake. Agent Parker's ID is valid, as is Agent Wolf's. There is no reason at all to arrest these people. The federal agents have everything under control. You will all return to your homes to rest. All except the sheriff, go now."*

They watched as the men all got in their cars and drove away. *"Now, Sheriff, you will return to your office and destroy any and all evidence you have against Agent Parker or the rest of our party. You will also delete any evidence or suspicions from your computers, as well as any notes you may have made. Should anyone ever ask, you made a mistake. Now go."*

The sheriff got back in his car without a word. Igor sighed as he watched the car drive away. "Marlene, my friend, you're amazing."

"Just make sure Lilly knows that at Christmas."

"She knows," chuckled Igor, "but I'll remind her anyway. So, now to deal with Derek."

"Please don't kill him, please."

"Jill, each time he does this he puts us all in grave danger. I can't spend months chasing him all over creation. This has to stop. Come on, Bran, we have to chase him down once again."

"Wait, I know where he'll go. Just please, let me talk to him, please."

Igor sighed and nodded. "I'm sorry, Jill, I'm just frustrated. I'm not going to kill Derek, but I have to take him to the king, and that I will do. If he won't come on his own accord, then I'll have to take him by force, but I swear to you I won't kill him.

"You say you know where he went. Where is that, and how fast can we get there?"

"The sheriff said they had a truck with Big Red's herd in it. That would be at the holding corral. He knows where that is and that's where he's gone. He's like you, Mr. Wolf. You'd go to save your pack and he'll go to save his herd."

"Take us there."

"Please, let me talk to him first, please."

"Da, it's best that you do, I need time to cool off. Larise, is everything we need in the cars?"

"Both cars are loaded, and the truck is ready too."

"Good, Merle, bring Larise and Marlene in your truck. Miss Peggy, go pack for yourself and Merle."

"Pack?"

"You heard the sheriff, too many people know wrong things. It's not safe for you here anymore. Come with us, we'll find a place for you."

"Merle?"

"He's right, Peggy. Even if there's no trouble, the damn bank will probably take the place anyway. These folks are offering us a chance, and we'll be with family. Let's go with them."

"Merle, what about our horses? We can't just turn them loose and I sure as hell won't sell a good saddle horse for dog food."

"Once we're on the road I'll call Elroy Baker and let him know where to find them. He's been wanting to add another trail ride anyway but couldn't afford the horses. He'll be happy enough to watch the place for us until we get things straightened out."

Peggy's shoulders sagged and she nodded. "I guess you're right, Merle. We should go. All right, young fella, you track down Big Red and we'll pack up."

AS THE CAR SPED ALONG with Jill at the wheel, Marlene leaned close to Igor. "You okay?"

"What? Oh sure, I'm fine, just a bit frustrated."

"That's not what I meant, and you know it."

Igor sighed and settled back in the seat. "I know. I'm okay."

"Bullshit."

"What can I do, Miss Marlene? This is the life I've chosen, the woman I've chosen. She's wild and free, and I have no right to try to tame her."

"So, you won't say anything?"

"Probably not."

"Then I will."

"Just let it go. It doesn't matter." Marlene didn't respond, she just patted his hand and gazed out the window.

"SALLY, ARE YOU SURE?"

"I am, Harald. This is it, Igor's right on the edge. If this goes wrong, he'll kill the were-horse, and Rhonda too, if she tries to stop him. The entire fate of all non-humans depends on what Rhonda does next. We need her and the were-horse to make an end of something. Dammit, I hate it when I can't see the outcomes."

"Sally?"

"It's because the situation is so volatile, Harald, the outcome is still in flux. That's why I can't see what happens. I'm going to look farther out into the future, maybe I can get a clue from there ..."

She fell silent as she allowed the trance to take her. The king sat brooding, waiting for her to return to him.

Sorting it Out

They arrived at a hill overlooking the holding corrals. Derek was there in human form, pacing around. Rhonda was trying to calm him. As they got out of the car they could hear him. "They're not here. They said the horses were here. Where could they be? What ..."

"Easy, Derek, easy," soothed Rhonda. "Look, Igor's here now, he'll know what to do." To her great surprise, Igor just looked away from her sadly.

"Igor?"

"I gotta find them." Derek transformed but barely took a step when Marlene's fist connected with his head and the mighty stallion stumbled and nearly fell.

"You stay put, or else," said Marlene. She moved past him and got between Rhonda and Igor. "We need to talk."

"Not now, Marlene." Rhonda tried to step past her. "Igor, honey?"

"Shut up, Rhonda. Follow me." Marlene led her a short distance from the others, then turned to face the rage in the Lady Hawk's eyes. *"You will be quiet until I've finished, then you may speak."*

Marlene sighed as she looked Rhonda in the eye. "Look, I know you're pissed, but you're so damned hard-headed, there was no other way to get you to listen. Ronni, you're on the edge of screwing up something beautiful. Igor loves

105

you deeply, madly, utterly, as only the wolf can, and you're throwing that away.

"For Christ's sake, you run around naked, flirting with every man around, and you've been all over Derek since we got here. Jesus, Ronni, Igor was facing men with guns, and you just took off after Derek. You should have been watching Igor's back, to hell with Derek. Igor's hurting and you're the cause of it."

She stopped speaking and glared at Rhonda whose face had gone from angry to distraught. "You may speak now."

"I swear to God, if you ever do that again ..."

"Oh stop being so damn thick-headed and think. I'm your friend here. You're on the edge of losing Igor, and your acting too much like a horny teenager to see it."

"For pity sake, Marlene. You, Bran, and Larise were with him. Hell, Igor could take those fools by himself. I was trying to keep the damned horse from getting away again."

Marlene sighed and reached out to lightly grip Rhonda's arm. "That's not what he saw, honey. Danger appeared, the other man ran like a rabbit, and you went with him. You've been all over him from the start."

"No, I ... dammit, I've just been trying to help him adjust, to convince him to come with us of his own free will. I'd never ... Igor knows better than that."

"Maybe in his head, girl, but not in his heart. Go on now, get that bare ass over there and make this right with your man."

"Marlene ..."

"Go."

Rhonda nodded and walked swiftly to where Igor and Bran had tied Derek with restraints. Igor was speaking as she reached them. "Don't try to transform to escape the bonds, Bran will be watching. I'm tired of your lack of self-control, and I'm tired of coddling you."

"And so am I," said Rhonda, as she reached them.

She linked her arm through Igor's and started to lead him away, but he pulled loose from her grip. "Not now, Rhonda, I have to ..."

"Talk to me, that's what you have to do. Bran, toss Derek in the car and head for the ranch. Send Larise back with the other car to fetch us. Marlene, please make sure Derek doesn't run off again."

"If he does, I'll go after him myself, and he won't like it. Come on, folks, we'll leave these two love birds here to sort themselves out." She herded them into the car then it drove away.

"Now you have nothing left to do except talk to me."

"I've got nothing to say."

"That's fair, I know. Igor, I messed up here, badly. I know that. Please just listen. Sweetheart, remember when we found Justine, how you called her your brave little mouse, your beautiful Justine."

"I explained ..."

Rhonda laid her finger on his lips to silence him. "Yes you did, lover, yes you did. Bear with me now. Remember how I got all messed up and angry because I thought you might want to use another woman to make pups.

"Igor, what I was feeling back then is what you're feeling now. None of what was going through my head back then was true or rational."

"And neither is this?"

"Remember how you held me close and made me understand it was me and only me you wanted? Please let me do the same for you.

"Igor, I don't want Derek, the man's a pain in the ass, he has no impulse control, and I'm desperately afraid the king will be forced to kill him to keep him quiet. I'm just trying to help him hold it together until we can get him back to the castle.

"I'm sorry if I gave you the wrong impression, neglected you, or made the wrong ..."

"You forgot one other thing from the Justine adventure, the most important thing of all."

"What was it? What did I forget? Please, just tell me how I can make this right."

"You can remember what you did back then."

"What I did?"

"To make me forget all my troubles and doubts, even my own name, to ..."

With a cry of delight Rhonda sealed his lips with a searing kiss. She held it, lingered and wallowed in it, pouring all her love and passion for him into it. "Oh god, Igor, I'm so sorry."

"Huh? What are you talking about, pretty lady? Who is Igor?"

Her laughter was sweet and rich as she hugged herself tightly to him. "Igor, I would never want anyone but you, ever. Sweetheart, I love you madly, you only, and I just want us to go home."

"Da, me too, Sweet Ronni. I hate this place, the heat, no trees, I too just want to go home. How are we going to get through to that damn fool horse?"

"Doesn't seem to have a lot of horse sense, does he?"

Igor laughed heartily at that. "No, my pretty bird, he surely doesn't."

"Oh, that's so much better," she sighed, as she cuddled deeper into his embrace.

"What's better?"

"I'm back to being your pretty bird instead of Rhonda. I like this a lot better."

"I'm sorry, Sweet Ronni."

"No love, I'm the one who's sorry. You were hurting and upset, and I was the cause of it. All better now?"

"All better now." He lifted his head to listen. "What is that?"

"It's a truck coming. I wonder ..."

"Want to go up for a look?"

"Be right back." She kissed his cheek then leaped skyward. Igor smiled as he watched her go. All was well in his world once more.

The hawk made several lazy circles as she watched the men unload the horses into a corral, then get into a car and drive away. She returned to Igor. "Yep, that's Derek's herd all right. I recognize two of them. What do you want to do, lover?"

"Those men are gone. Want to load the horses back onto the truck and drive it away?"

"Can you drive that monster?"

"Da, Eric taught me. Come on, this will be fun."

It wasn't as easy as they'd hoped. The horses were in no hurry to get back into the truck. Eventually, Igor went wolf and began to circle the corral. That did the trick. As soon as the last horse was in the truck, Rhonda closed the gate as Igor morphed back and pulled on his clothes.

They were just climbing into the truck when Larise arrived. "Head back," shouted Igor. "Tell Derek we're bringing his herd. Larise, see if you can contact the king and make some arrangements to transport all the horses. I don't want to drive this stolen truck all the way back to the Lair."

"On it," she sang, as she tooted the horn and sped away again. Igor revved the engine a bit then ground the gears a few times, but he got them rolling. Rhonda sat grinning in the passenger's seat, dressed only in Igor's t-shirt.

"What's going on?" asked Derek, as Marlene cut his bonds to set him free. "First you try to break my jaw, then you cut me loose?"

"First," she said coolly, "if I wanted to break your jaw, it would have been broken. That was just a tap to slow you down, so you couldn't run away again. Second, I believe that impulse to run belongs to the horse, but you need to get a grip on it and fast.

"Third, that's your woman standing right there, keep your eyes off the Lady Hawk before Igor gets pissed. There is a way to make an immortal stay dead, and Igor is well versed in the technique."

"What? No, good god, no. Jill's my girl, my one and only. What the hell are you people thinking?"

"Look at her face, buddy. Tell me I'm wrong."

Derek turned to Jill, but she averted her gaze and stepped away. "Jill, wait. Dammit, wait. Jill, whatever you think, or whatever you think you saw, it's not true. You ..."

"She's been all over you, and you can't take your eyes off her, Derek. Shit, I might as well not even be here at all."

"Jill, that's not true. Rhonda's just trying to help me adjust to what's happened, she ..."

"That's my job. I'm the one you're supposed to turn to. I'm the one who's supposed to ..." She stopped speaking and burst into tears.

He stepped closer to take her in his arms, but she jerked out of his grasp. "No, dammit, don't touch me."

"Jill, dammit all to hell, will you please listen? I love you, only you."

"Then why the hell do you keep running away from me?"

"Running away from you? Is that what you think I'm doing? Jill, that's not me, it's the stallion, and he's running back to his herd to protect them. When that need takes him it hits so fast I can't control it."

"Well, you'd damn well better learn," growled Merle, "or those two werewolves will rip you apart. That boy has a world of patience, but he's running out. You run off on him again and he's likely to make an end of you. Now you get a grip, for Jill's sake if not your own."

At this point Marlene dropped her phone back into her pocket, a bemused grin on her face. "Listen up, people. Igor and Ronni are on their way back with Derek's herd. Apparently, they stole the truck."

"The herd? They've got the herd?" Derek turned to Jill, and she was startled to see the excitement in his eyes.

"Oh my god," she breathed. "Look at you. It's all true, isn't it? You're able to hold your human form now, but you're still more Big Red than Derek."

"Jill, please, I ..."

"No. No, Derek. The wolves mate for life, but that damned horse doesn't. He needs a herd of mares. I can tell you right now, mister, I'll never be part of your herd. You might want a harem now, but I'll never be a part of it." She turned and ran.

Igor arrived shortly after that. "Derek, you're still here. Good. I know what's going on for you now. It's not you running away, it's your horse nature. The animal impulse is still too strong for you to control. The stallion wants to protect his herd. The herd is here now, so you and all of us can protect them and take them with us to safety."

Igor stoped speaking as he saw their faces. "What is it? What's wrong now?"

"Now Jill ran away," sighed Peggy.

"Oh for the love of ..."

"Easy lover, easy, I'll find her." Rhonda leaped into the sky and Igor caught the falling t-shirt then pulled it over his head.

"Larise?"

"Igor, the king says to head for the rail yard in Riverside Junction. There'll be a rail car waiting for us. We'll put the horses on the train and we can pick them up again when we reach New York where Eric will meet us with another truck."

"Good. Let's get ready so we can leave as soon as Ronni and Jill get back.

Jillian was behind the old barn, leaning on a corral rail, weeping softly. She sighed deeply as she heard the soft flutter of wings then sensed a presence beside her. "Great," she muttered. "Go away, Rhonda. I'm not in the mood right now."

"Sucks, doesn't it, Jill."

"What the hell are you talking about?"

"When your man is all over another woman, or it looks like he is."

"How would you know?"

"Been there, done that, got the t-shirt."

"Yeah? Then why the hell won't you ever wear it?"

That brought a howl of laughter from the Lady Hawk, and Jill grinned in spite of herself. "Rhonda, all the men go half blind and start drooling whenever you're around. What the hell would you know about a guy with a wandering eye?"

"Igor and I were all brand new when he rescued a were-mouse. She was caught halfway through the change. He called her his brave little mouse, his courageous Justine, and cuddled her close all the time to protect and reassure her. He says he was just being a protective alpha. What I saw was something quite different.

"You see, I knew her. Justine is drop dead gorgeous, and I knew that as soon as she mastered the change ... Well, you get the idea. I went super bitch all over the poor guy. It wasn't pretty, but we managed to sort it out. Turns out he really was just being a protective alpha.

"Now that brings me to the point. Derek has gained enough control to hold his human form, but the stallion's responses are still too strong for him to control. He needs time to work on that, and he needs motivation."

"Motivation?"

"You, Jill. What you're seeing is me chasing him down and him getting all gooey-eyed when I get near. That's the stallion, wants every available mare it sees, can't help itself and doesn't want to. Believe me, I'm not interested. Igor's my guy all the way.

"I keep going after Derek because I'm the only one fast enough to catch him, and I'm not a natural predator so I won't scare him to death, but frankly, it's pissing me off. If he takes off and runs afoul of horse thieves who discover what he is, then the jig's up. It'll have to be cleaned up, there'll be a bloodbath, and Derek will be among the dead."

"You people said he's immortal."

"He is, but there's a way to make an immortal stay dead, and Igor has done it before. Jill, there's still time to salvage this, to keep Derek alive and get a happy ending to this mad adventure, but it's in your hands now."

"My hands? What can I do? I've already lost him."

"Honey, the only thing you've lost is your confidence. Your man's back there wondering what the hell's going on."

"Yes, and If I go back it won't be ten minutes before he runs off again."

"Girl, you need to tame that horse, break him to the saddle, get a bridle on him, and take control."

"And how do you suggest I do that with you running around naked all the time? Jesus, Rhonda, you're so gorgeous, and all the men fall all over you. They don't even know I'm there."

"So, remind them. Look, you go back. There's a wrap dress and sandals in the back of that car. You get the dress out and I'll land in it. I'll find a way to stay covered up until this adventure's over, but you'll have to help me. Now, go back there and take that man by the ear and fix this."

Jill squared her shoulders and straightened up. "All right, I'll try. Rhonda ..."

"Ronni, please. People only call me Rhonda when they're pissed at me." Grinning, she leaped into the sky.

The hawk circled lazily overhead. "What the hell's going on?" grumbled Merle. "She needs to get down here, so we can get going."

"She's waiting for something," replied Igor.

"She's waiting for me," said Jill, as she strode from behind the barn.

Derek stepped toward her. "Jill ..."

"We need to talk, but not now, and not with an audience," she said, as she brushed past him.

She found the dress and sandals in the car and held the dress up. The hawk swooped in then transformed almost inside it. She swept it around her body, and winked at Jill as she tied the belt at her waist. "Come on people, we need to get on the road. Mount up."

Queen Sally sighed and leaned back against the king's shoulder. "I believe I have underestimated our Lady Hawk, and her devotion to Igor. The worst is over with that, and now we're down to the were-horse. It's now up to Mr. Wheeler to gain control of the horse's impulses. If he can manage it, we have a strong chance of defeating this crisis."

On the Road

It was a strange looking convoy. Igor was driving the big rig with the horses in the back, Rhonda riding shotgun and reading the map. Behind him was Derek's old truck with him and Jill, followed by Merle and Peggy, with Branimir, Larise, and Marlene bringing up the rear.

As he drove, Derek kept his eye on the herd of horses in the back of the big truck. He'd given up on trying to get Jill to talk to him. Finally, she sighed and spoke.

"Derek, I need you to listen to me, please."

"I'm all ears."

"No, you're not, and that's the problem. Derek, you've managed to gain control of your physical form, but the horse is still running the show. Please listen to me."

"All right, Jill, I'm listening."

"Okay, first, I need you to fully understand that I love you, heart and soul."

"Jill, I love you too. There's never been any other woman for me, you know that. Since the first time I laid eyes on you there's never been anyone else for me."

118

"I feel the same, Derek, so please hold that in mind and listen to me."

"Okay, honey, I'm listening."

"Derek, something happened to blend you with that horse. My attempts to learn how to help you drew the attention of the vampire king. He sent a team to help us because of my sister."

"I know. What's your point?"

"Just shut the hell up and listen. Up there, driving that truck, is a werewolf who can easily make a permanent end of you, of both of us. At the back of the line is a vampire who can make anybody do anything she wants, and she takes her orders from the werewolf."

"Jill for the love of god, what are you driving at?"

"Derek, what they're seeing is you running off at the drop of a hat and Rhonda chasing after you. They're also seeing you drool every time she gets near you."

"What??? Jill ..."

"Just shut up and listen. I know that's not you, it's the damned stallion. You can hold your human form, but you can't control his impulses. However, that's what they're seeing, and it's pissing Rhonda off. Worse, it's making Igor jealous. Derek, you and I both know that king gave Igor the power to make the big decision, help us or make us vanish forever.

"Derek, please get it through your thick head, all our lives depend on you getting control of that horse inside you."

"All our lives?"

"You, me, Peggy, and Merle, we all know too much. Come on, lover, use your head. Derek, you've always been a thinker. Think first, act second, but now you just ..." She stopped talking and burst into tears.

"Jill, please don't cry. Do you really think they would ..."?

"They can't have loose ends, Derek. Think about it," she sniffed.

"Sweet Jesus," he sighed. "Okay, help me here, what do I do?"

"Stop acting like a stallion in heat and act like a man, a man who promised to love me and only me for the rest of his life."

Derek was silent for several moments, his thoughts racing. "Jill, I'll need your help here. Don't hold back and don't wait. If I screw up, tell me and don't be shy about it. Jill, I do love you, only you. I need you to know that. I swear I'll do whatever it takes to prove that to you, to everybody."

"Then be the man, Derek, tame the horse. Break him to the saddle."

"He's quiet inside me now, Jill. He can see the herd and he knows it's safe, so he's quiet."

"For now."

"For now, but his instinctive drives are so damn strong, and so instant. For an animal to survive in the wild they can't stop to think every action through, they just act. The stronger that drive is, the more likely they are to survive."

"Then you have to overcome that instinct, just like any other horse wrangler. You've got to gain that animal's trust and break him to the saddle for all our sakes. And for god's sake, stop drooling over Rhonda."

"Dammit, Jill, I don't drool over Rhonda. Cripes, she runs around naked all the time, and you won't touch me anymore, what the hell am I ...?"

"I won't touch you?"

"Not since they showed up," he sighed. "The only time you've touched me since then is when I'm the horse."

"Derek?"

"Look, I get it, you're scared, this whole thing is scary as hell, but I need you, Jill. I need you to help me, I need you to stop holding back from me. If I ever hope to get control of this thing then I need your support, I need to know you still love me, and I need to know you're not afraid of me.

"This will take both of us if it's to work. Hell, if I'm losing you, then I really don't care anyway."

Jillian gazed at him for a long moment then unclipped her seatbelt and slid over tight to his side, snuggling under his arm. "You're not losing me, you big dummy, I was just scared I was losing you."

"That'll never happen, Jill, you know that."

"I was secure in that with the old Derek, but you're something new, something with the instinct to claim a harem."

"No, girl, no harem, just you. Big Red has his harem right up there in that truck, but the only woman I want is right here in my arms. Stop holding back, get tough, nag, henpeck, and whatever else you have to do, but keep me on the straight and narrow. Promise me now, Jill. Promise you'll never leave me."

"I promise, Derek. If you need me to be lead mare until you get control of this, then that's who I'll be."

"That's what I need. I think Big Red will accept that too. For some reason, I think he will accept that and follow your lead. Oh, and keep a blanket handy."

"A blanket?"

"To throw over Lady Hawk."

Jill laughed at that. "Maybe I'll just put blinders on you, buddy." He sighed and hugged her closer. The tear in his world had finally been mended.

They stopped for lunch and Igor nodded his approval as he watched Jill and Derek walk to the roadside café, arm in arm. "Now that's a lot better."

"Second that," grinned Rhonda, as she linked her arm through his and followed the others.

After lunch they set out again, but disaster soon struck. A pick-up truck coming the other way blew a tire and crashed into the truck loaded with Derek's herd. Igor fought the truck to a stop and leaped down to the ground. The back doors had popped open; the horses jumped down and raced away.

Derek leaped from the old truck, but Jill grabbed him and jerked him to a stop. "Don't even think about it, mister. Get your ass into that old horse trailer of Merle's and help me with Big Red. I've got to catch that herd."

With a quick nod, he grabbed her hand and sprinted for the trailer hooked to his truck. Once inside and out of sight of strangers, he transformed, and she put a bridle on him. The stallion didn't like it, but Derek fought him, and he stood quivering.

Jill backed him out of the trailer then leaped onto his back. The stallion gave a few dancing steps then raced away after the herd, Jill clinging to his back.

"Ronni?"

"Naw, she's got this, Igor. Come on, we have to see to those folks and make sure our truck is fit to drive." He nodded and followed her to where the other truck had come to a stop in the ditch. Merle was already there with the older couple.

"Everybody okay here?" asked Igor.

"Yeah, we're all right," replied the man. "Dang tire blew, and I lost control. Sorry your horses got away."

"Forget it. Jill will bring them back."

"That gal only had a bridle on that stallion."

"That's all she needs," grinned Merle. "I think we can get the spare on for you right where she sits. With that tire on we can pull you out and you can be on your way."

"As long as I didn't mess anything else up."

While the men looked over the situation, Rhonda approached the woman who'd been a passenger in the pick-up. "That's a nasty bump you've got on your noggin. Can I take a look at it?"

"You a doctor, young miss?"

"Dr. Rhonda Stockman, at your service, ma'am."

"Well, okay then, I guess."

Rhonda gently felt around the woman's head, then gazed into her eyes for a long moment. "Looks okay to me, but you should get checked out as soon as you can get to your family doctor."

"I'll do that, and thanks. Wait a minute, you're a veterinarian, aren't you?"

"Busted," laughed Rhonda. "How'd you guess?"

"All the horses. Ah, what the hell, you're probably smarter that that lot at the hospital anyway."

"Thanks, but I'd get that checked just in case, just to be sure."

"I will. All your folks okay?"

"Looks like. Come on, I'll see if I can find you a few pain killers in one of the cars."

While everyone back at the roadway sorted themselves out, Jillian was having her own difficulties. She'd just spotted the runaway herd when the stallion suddenly bucked her off and started to run away. With a yelp of surprise, she tried to roll with the fall.

He only managed a few steps before shimmering into Derek who ran to Jill's side, the bridle dangling foolishly from his neck. "Jill, honey, are you all right?"

She struggled to her feet and took a limping step, then beat the dust off her jeans. "You bucked me off? What the hell was that about?"

"Jill, I'm so sorry, I am. It was Big Red. He wants to lead the herd away, he doesn't like them in the truck, confined."

"Sonofabitch, Derek. That hurt." She took another limping step. "Look, I don't care what that damned horse wants. Igor will slaughter the lot of them and you too if you try that. Get a grip on that damned horse."

"I'm trying, Jill. I swear I'm trying," he said as he tossed aside the bridle.

"Bullshit, Derek. You toss me off again and I swear I'll ask Rhonda to geld you. I mean it. Now you transform back and get a grip on that animal part of your nature. We're going back without them."

"What? No, Jill, I, we can't ..."

"Yes you fucking can, but you don't want to. Well I'm done. I'll walk back alone if I have to, but I'm through with this. Everybody has gone the extra mile for you, now it's your turn to man up. If I go back alone the werewolves and vampire will come for you. It won't be Rhonda's bare ass and soft voice this time, it'll be Igor fangs and Marlene's claws."

"Jill ..."

She didn't reply, she just limped away. She heard the stallion bugle once behind her then silence. A few more steps and she felt a soft nudge at her backside. "Piss off, Derek."

Another gentle nudge and a soft snort, then a soft nose brushed her neck. In spite of herself, Jill had to laugh. "Stop it, I'm mad at you." Another gentle nudge. "Quit it."

"Jill honey, don't be mad. Red's sorry, and so am I."

She turned to glare at him, but stopped and stared. Derek was there, and so was the herd, all lined up behind him. He transformed to the horse again and knelt for her to mount. Grinning in spite of herself, she grabbed a handful of his mane and swung her leg across his back. "You buck me off again and I swear I'll kick your sorry ass all the way back to the truck."

Big Red rose up, snorted once, and then set out at a gentle trot. To Jill's great surprise the rest of the herd followed along.

Damage Control

While Jillian brought the horses back to the truck, Terry Sawchuk, the Vampire king's top agent, was in a private meeting with the director of a secret government agency. Director Bridger sat in his office, facing a man who was once his partner.

"All right, Terry, what the hell's going on? I've got people from three different departments digging into my business, red flags going up all over the place, and it's going to be a nightmare to smooth over."

"I did ask you to leave Larise Parker on the books, Egan."

"Why the hell should I? She works for you now. So, she tried to scam a local sheriff out west, and he got wise, is that it?"

"That was the tip of the iceberg, yeah."

"Tip of the iceberg?"

"Yeah. That sheriff's brother-in-law was an independent consultant for the FBI, a computer geek. Anyway, the sheriff asked him to poke around, and he got real enthusiastic about it."

"I know. He hacked into our database, searched a lot of top level files he shouldn't have been able to access, and more. He hit Homeland Security and the CIA as well. The little bastard got into all sorts of top level stuff. Now everybody is after my head because it was one of my former agents that set it off. They want me to terminate the guy."

"Not necessary, Egan. Our people already had a chat with him."

"Let me guess, your wife?"

"Her sister."

"She has a sister? Is she anything like your better half?"

"Worse."

"Okay, so that threat's been neutralized. Fine. Why the hell were your people out there anyway?"

"There was an incident."

"Incident?"

"More of that green shit appeared with predictable results. Our people were on the scene fast, but the local sheriff got too nosy. Suspicious bugger. Anyway, with Larise showing a dead badge, well, you can see how that went. We caught on and neutralized the hacker, but he stirred up a lot of interest."

"Yeah, he sure did, goddam hackers anyway. So, I ask again, what do you need from me?"

"I need a clean badge for Larise."

"Can't do it, Terry. I can't. Since that damned hacker stirred up all the shit I've got overseers and auditors crawling all over me. I can't do it."

"Okay, give me the names of the overseers and auditors."

"What??? Are you out of your fucking mind? I can't tell you any of that. Christ, if they thought I did that I'd be tossed in a hole so deep sunlight couldn't find me at the bottom." He got up and paced around for a moment then grabbed Terry's hat off the desk where he'd dropped it. "Here's your hat, now get the hell out of my office."

Without another word, Terry accepted the hat and walked out of the room. Outside, a tall blonde linked her arm through his and picked the information stick from the hat. She kissed his cheek, deposited the hat onto his head, and dropped the info drive into her own pocket.

That night several people were visited by vampires. The next day, Director Bridger was given a clean report, and the overseers took the auditors away with them. Agent Larise Parker's new badge was delivered to Terry Sawchuk at his hotel that afternoon.

"It's all good, Sire," said Terry, as he reported to the king. "Miss Gina and Gudrun paid a few discreet visits to key people last night, and Egan's in the clear. His people are busy erasing the trail left by the hacker, and shutting down any undue interest. We're fine on that score."

"Good to know, Terry. If you're clear, then come on home." The king dropped his phone back into his pocket and sighed. "Now if Igor can just bring that damned horse here without any further misadventures."

It wasn't going to be that easy. Someone had spotted the accident and called it in to the Highway Patrol. They'd been given the license number of the big truck and it was registered as a stolen vehicle. The old couple in the damaged pick-up were just driving away as the Highway Patrol came in sight.

"Well, shit, can anything else go wrong?" grumbled Igor, as the police car lit up with flashing lights.

"Here we go again," grinned Rhonda. "Let me, sweetheart."

"Be my guest, my pretty bird."

"Afternoon folks," called the officer, as he stepped from the car with his gun drawn. "Ya'll step out with your hands in the air, now. Nobody needs to get hurt."

"Actually, Officer," said Rhonda, as she stepped towards him, "I'm a little disappointed that you start a conversation with gun drawn rather than ask if everybody is all right."

"My apologies, Ma'am, but I'm a cautious man. You folks were reported as having an accident, and that is a stolen truck."

"I'm not arguing any of that," she replied, taking another step toward him. "I caution you, Officer, don't get any closer to the truck. We've all been immunized, but you haven't. We did disinfect the truck, but can't be too careful, you know."

"Just who the hell are you people?"

"Federal agents. I'm Dr. Rhonda Stockman, veterinarian, and this is Agent Wolf. He's in charge of this case." Igor held up his badge, so the policeman could see it. The man squinted at it then lowered his weapon.

"Now, Officer, a couple of years ago, a disgruntled employee of a government lab released something he shouldn't have as he quit and left the building. That mess was cleared up eventually, but he disappeared with more of the toxin.

"We tracked him to this area, and found he'd been experimenting on wild horses. No idea why. That man has been stopped and dealt with, but the herd he infected was on the loose. We managed to maneuver them into an enclosed area, but as usual things went sideways.

"The man escaped, convinced the local sheriff we were horse thieves, and the herd was captured by rustlers before we could straighten things out. We managed to regain the herd and decided to use the rustler's truck since the horses were already aboard."

"Ah-huh. I don't see any horses in that rig. I suppose they ran away."

"They did, but one of our people went to retrieve them. Here she comes now with the herd."

He turned to see Jill, mounted bareback on the stallion, leading the small herd towards the roadway. Merle wrestled the ramp into position and Jill led them up into the back of the trailer. Once the horses were loaded Jill led the stallion down the ramp and Merle closed up the back of the truck.

Jill loaded the stallion into the small horse trailer then joined the others.

"I thought you said those were wild horses," said the policeman.

"They are," said Jill, "but I've been out on the plains with that herd for a long time. They trust me, hell, even the stallion lets me ride him."

"Look, Officer, are we done here?" asked Igor. "I'd really like to get on the road."

"It's not that I don't believe your story, Agent Wolf, but I have a problem here."

"And that is?"

"That truck was reported stolen, and I've informed dispatch that I've seen it. We've also been on the video recorder since I got out of the car. How am I supposed to just let you drive away?"

"Marlene?"

"Yes, Igor?"

"Would you be kind enough to answer this man's question for him?"

"I'd be delighted," grinned the cute redhead who had caught the officer's eye. "It's like this officer. *Obey me! Stand still and do not speak.*"

The man swallowed hard, trembling in fear. That wasn't a human voice, it was the voice of a demon from hell. Worse, he was unable to disobey it in any way.

"What these people have told you is true. You believe this utterly. Also, the license plate from this truck has obviously been changed with another vehicle. You will radio in that this plate was swapped out, and let these people go about their business. These federal agents are not to be interfered with in any way.

"All you will remember about this is the red-haired girl was extremely attractive, especially the freckles on her nose. You will now send us on our way and return to your duties."

She was smiling at him wickedly as he shook off the spell. Blushing furiously, he turned to Igor who passed him the license plate. "You folks go on now. You can pick up a replacement plate in the next town." He gave Marlene a long look as he returned to his own car and drove away.

Grinning, Marlene turned to see Merle looking at her. "What?"

"What? You're as shameless as the rest of them."

Marlene's grin just broadened. "Merle, my old darling, you ain't seen nothing yet. Just wait until you meet Gudrun."

"Better toughen up, Merle," grinned Peggy.

"Woman, don't you even start. You've been hanging out with this bunch too long already."

Once the police car was out of sight, Derek came out of the trailer to join the others.

On the Road

"There we go, all set, Agent Wolf. We'll make sure they have feed and water. They'll arrive in New York in four days."

"Maybe I should travel with them," said Derek.

"There's no need, sir," replied the railway worker. "We've transported plenty of livestock. They'll be fine."

"They're not fucking livestock," snarled Derek, as he took a step toward the man.

Jillian got between them instantly, facing Derek. "Back off. This man knows his job and he didn't mean anything by what he said." She turned to face the startled worker. "I'm sorry, sir. Derek's just overtired. It took us weeks to bring in this small herd and we're beat. These horses are wild mustangs, headed for a reserve back east."

She turned back and took Derek by the arm. "Come on, sweetheart, you need a good meal and a week of sleep, you'll be fine." She led him away toward the truck while Igor made the final arrangements.

Derek leaned against the bed of his pickup truck and sighed deeply. Jill followed and put her hand on his shoulder. "Derek?"

"Sorry I went all nasty on that guy. You're right, Jill. That damned horse has no impulse control at all. He's never had need of it, quite the opposite. I have to get a grip on that, and I'm trying, but it sure isn't easy."

"If it was easy then anybody could do it," grinned Branimir, as he leaned against the tailgate. "This is the part where you decide who you will become. Will you spend the rest of forever being a horse's ass, or will you rise up, take control, and be the rider, the cowboy who rides the horse?"

"You know, Bran, the thing I like about you best is the way you're always so diplomatic."

Branimir chuckled at that. "Derek, my friend, we tried being nice to you, but it didn't work. You're a lazy bugger, you just sat back and let the horse run the show. You know the trouble that caused. Now, it's time to man up and take control."

"How, Bran? How do I do that. I don't believe in breaking a horse. I earn their trust, make friends with them until they trust me enough to let me ride."

"Yeah? How's that working for you this time?"

"Not so great. Dammit all anyway, why the hell did I have to get blended with that horse."

"He's a tough case?"

"Bran, I can't begin to tell you how wild and fierce that horse is. I try to push him down, but something happens and he takes over."

Grinning, Branimir gave his shoulder a friendly clap. "The horse scares you, doesn't he?"

"Yeah, he does."

Jillian shook her head at that. "Then why the hell did you not stay back and wait for me. What in god's name possessed you try to cut him loose yourself?"

Derek turned to face her. "Because I couldn't stand to see him brought down. They might have wanted to put him down, or maybe to tame him. That creature is magnificent, wild and free as the wind."

"So, you don't really want to tame him," said Igor as he and Rhonda joined them.

"No, but I know I have to if I'm going to survive, if I want him to survive. The trouble is, he knows we're in danger. His natural response to that is to run, race the wind."

"So, what do you plan to do?" asked Igor as he and Rhonda joined the group.

"I've already done it."

The grin on Derek's face made Igor laugh. "You seem pretty pleased with yourself. Tell us what you've done."

"I've done something the horse will understand. I submitted to a stronger horse."

"Explain."

"I told Jill to take over and I just submit to her decisions. She's the lead mare now and Big Red understands how that works. Jill leads and we follow."

"That's it?"

"That's it, Igor. Look, the herd is on that train and pulling away, confined in a boxcar, but I'm still here. See me looking to Jill constantly? That's the horse asking why she won't go after them to set them free. She's not moving, so he accepts that she knows what she's doing, even if he doesn't understand it."

"Think it'll last?"

"It will, but I only need a few months to get full control of this. In a few months I'll have won him over, gained his full trust, and no more problem."

"You're sure."

"I am, Igor. I may be a stubborn fool, and a lazy bugger as Bran says, but I know horses. In a few months that horse will be as strong and fierce as ever, but he'll let me take the lead."

"So, you're saying that by trying to speed up the process, we were just screwing it up?"

"Somewhat. Why are you in such a hurry, anyway?"

Igor sighed and shook his head. "I guess it looks that way to you, and the horse. I just want to get you out of the possible public eye, into the presence of the king. Back at the Lair you can work your magic at your leisure, safe from prying eyes.

Even if someone does discover you there, we have people to address that, to protect you. Out here in the open, you'd be too vulnerable."

"Out here? Right, wolf, you like the forests better."

"Da, give me trees and cool shade."

"Not me. Give me wide open skies and a good horse. Add in Jill and my life is perfect. That's all I ever wanted, that's all I want now."

"So, work on your sales pitch," grinned Larise. "Don't try to rush it, but work on it. The king's a reasonable man. Make it good and he might let you return."

"It's not the king he has to convince," grinned Igor. "It's Queen Sally. If it sounds all right to the king, he will ask the queen before making a final decision. You won't be able to fool Queen Sally. She'll know if you truly have things under control, if it's safe to let you return.

"Enough of this now. The horses are gone, and we must go as well. Miss Marlene, do you want to take the rental car back then catch a plane home?"

"I'm good Igor. I'll see the mission through with you. Come on, let's get on the road."

"So, we're really driving back?"

"Yes, my pretty bird, Derek still doesn't have full control, and I don't want him in the plane until he does. I wish he'd ride in the trailer, but, sometimes you have to give a little."

"That makes sense, my love. Okay, let's go. You drive and I'll be the navigator."

The king relaxed in his favorite chair in the great hall. A large mug of coffee appeared at his right hand and he smiled as he thanked the girl, but she didn't seem to hear him. "Elaine?"

"Huh? Oh, sorry Sire, sorry. Did you ...?"

"Relax, Elaine. It's just that you seem distracted. Is there anything I can do?"

"Oh no, Sire, I just ..."

"Worried about your sister?"

"Yeah, Jill and the others."

"The others?"

"Merle and Peggy, mostly. I know you'll look after them, but they're a pair of independent thinkers."

The king smiled as he pushed a chair toward her. "Sit with me, Elaine. Tell me about them."

She thanked him and sat, folding her hands in her lap. "Well, they were our closest neighbors when I was young. They had no children of their own and we often hung out at their ranch. Once Mom died and Dad hit the bottle, Jill spent most of her time there.

"Everybody told me I had to be the woman of the family and help raise my younger sister, but she was too headstrong, and I was too confused. I couldn't do it, couldn't take over and be the grownup. I freaked out and ran away.

"Jill practically moved in with Merle and Peg. Merle is all bluster and heart, a big teddy bear. Peggy is the organized one, the take charge woman. She'd have been a great mom. Anyway, they took Jill in and made sure she stayed in school, stuff like that. They put me back together a few times as well.

"I feel so bad for them."

"Oh? Why?"

"I could tell by the look of the place, they're on the edge of losing the ranch. It's looking pretty run down. Everything they had was tied up in that old place.

"Fair warning, Sire. Jill wanted to keep Derek on that ranch. They're both all about horses, saving the wild horses. She wanted to keep him there to nurse him through the change. She'll try to talk you into letting them go back there."

He smiled again and nodded. "Fairly warned. So, you think the ranch is in financial trouble, but Jillian will be fixated on returning, is that it?"

"In a nutshell, Sire."

"Elaine, tell me more about Derek, how well do you know him?"

"Sire?"

"If I let them return, can he be trusted to stay out of the public eye? Will he stay focused on remaining unknown, or will he get complacent over time and get sloppy?"

Elaine smiled as she replied. "Oh, he'll stay out of the public eye all right. Derek's an intensely private person, introverted, doesn't want anybody knowing his business, doesn't trust easily. He'll stay focused, I'm sure of that.

"It's Jill who needs to fully understand the implications of being discovered. Derek will follow her lead all the way when the chips are down. He always has."

The king thought for a moment then nodded his head. "All right then. Tommy."

"Sire?"

"Get me the financials on that ranch of Elaine's friends. Now, Elaine, tell me what's likely to happen if I send these people back to the west."

"They'll go back to what they were doing, Jill and Derek working to save the wild mustangs, Peggy and Merle trying to keep that old horse ranch going by breeding and training saddle horses for the locals and trail ride companies."

"It doesn't sound like such a bad life at that," smiled the king. "I've spent a few generations leading a quiet life and enjoyed it."

"I've got the information now, Sire," said Tommy. "They've missed too many mortgage payments, and the bank is foreclosing. It'll go up for sale."

The king thought for a moment. "Watch it closely, Tommy. As soon as it hits the market, buy it."

"Yes sir, setting it up as we speak."

"Thank you, Tommy. Elaine, not a word of this to anyone except the queen."

Elaine was grinning with delight, she would have a few weeks to spend with her sister, and then Jill would have the life she wanted. "Lips are sealed, Sire. I'll get that refill on the coffee for you now."

As she walked away the king looked into his coffee mug and saw that it was empty. "Some days that girl scares me," he mused.

While the king enjoyed his coffee, Igor led his small group along the interstate highway. As the miles rolled by Derek relaxed more and more. He noticed Jill smiling at him as he drove along. "What?" he asked, with a smile of his own.

"You, it's suddenly like you're back to your old self."

"Getting there. Guess I put everybody through the wringer, didn't I?"

"Not you, Big Red. So, how's he doing?"

"He's fine. You're here, you're relaxed, and so he is too. You're the lead mare now, and he's fine with that. It's not about control for him. He lost the leadership of the herd, and he's okay."

"Really?"

"Yeah, it was tough when the other herd was here, but they're gone now, and this is a new herd. All the new people mess with him a bit, but as long as you're calm, he's good."

"When did this all happen?"

"When you walked away from us, Jill. He felt the loss in my soul, and it broke him. He realized at that point that he was stuck with me forever, and he couldn't face my pain at the loss of you.

"I know it looks like I'm just driving along, but I'm really working on Big Red too. Honey, give me a couple of months and this'll never be a problem again. As Bran says, I'll be Derek no matter what form I take. The horse's instincts will remain, but his impulses won't be able to overpower me anymore."

"Derek, what are you up to?"

"I haven't given up on our dream, Jill. Not for a single moment, but life threw us a curve. Now I'm half horse, and that brought the agents of a king we knew nothing about. Now we'll have to convince this king that it's safe to let us go home."

"Do you think we can?"

"Rhonda says he's a reasonable man, Igor agrees. This man has the unenviable task of keeping a whole range of people away from the public eye. If I can demonstrate that I have full control, and that I'm as adamant about keeping out of sight as he is, I have to believe we have a chance. I've been at this since I first met these folk."

"You have? Then why the hell have you been so dammed determined to drive them crazy? Rhonda was ready to throttle you, and Igor, god knows what held him back."

"I know."

"Then why?"

"It wasn't me. I was trying to get control of the damned horse, but every time I got close something would spook him and away we went. Jesus. That last round I nearly had him then he suddenly bucked you off.

"I freaked and he was ready to take me on, but you walked away, and he knew he had no choice. Those animal urges are pulling back now, Jill."

"Until something else goes sideways. Look, you're all relaxed now, but if we blow a tire, or somebody hits us, are you sure you can keep the horse from changing your form and trying to flee?"

"I'm sure."

"What if I freak out? Will he try to take over then?"

"No. We've got him in unfamiliar territory now. The only things familiar to him now are this new herd, you, Igor, and the rest. He'll look to the others for direction, he'll look to me.

"Look, I'll be the first to admit this would have been a lot easier if I was a natural dominant personality, but I'm not, and that's what's caused the problems; Big Red is or was."

"Was?"

"His consciousness is fading, Jill. He's slowly giving way, first to you, and now to me. I just need a few more weeks. He'll fade away, and I'll be me, man or horse." Derek's assessment was soon to be tested.

Hunted

It was midafternoon when Igor spotted the old motel. It was still early, but he was tired, they all were, and the motel looked good, so he pulled in with the others close behind. "I'll go see if they have room for us all," said Rhonda, as she hopped from the car and ran to the office. The others slowly climbed out of their vehicles and stretched out the kinks.

A few moments later she returned with five sets of keys and began passing them out. "Okay, here we go, folks, Merle, Larise, Marlene, Jill, and I've got ours. There's a café down that way where we can get a meal."

"Works for me," said Igor, as he got the number from the key she handed him. "Eighteen, eighteen, ah, down near the end. Bring the car, Bran, and we'll unload." He tossed Branimir the car keys then started walking toward the end of the row.

An hour and a half later they were returning from the café when two men burst from one of the rooms. The thieves spotted the group and pulled their guns and fired. They leaped aboard their ATVs and raced away down a dirt road that disappeared into the forest. Two huge wolves were hard after them, and the hawk was already in the air.

148

Derek hesitated for only a moment then he acted. "Marlene, mount up and hang on."

Startled, Marlene spun to face him. He shifted into the horse and leaped toward her. As he sped past she grabbed a fistful of his mane and swung aboard his back. She leaned forward as he raced after the wolves.

Jill looked startled. "What the hell just happened?"

"At first glance, I'd say your man ran off with another woman, again," grinned Larise.

"That's getting old really fast."

"Take another look at it, Jill."

"Another look?"

"Two men with guns, two wolves in pursuit. Derek knows both he and Marlene are immortal, Igor and Bran aren't. He also knows what she's capable of. If he can get her past the wolves, she can have those men down before the boys get there."

"Yeah, I guess. That's the sort of thing Derek would do. Do you think that's what happened?"

"I do. Come on folks, it's up to us to see if anything important is missing. We need to know if those fools are just a couple of dumbass burglars, or if they're something more sinister."

While Larise and friends took inventory of the damage, Big Red was closing fast on the wolves. The road roughened and turned into a rocky trail as it wound its way up a hill. As the wolves crested the hill the horse blew past them and hurtled down the slope at breakneck speed.

The road turned back into the forest, and as the wolves made the turn they found Derek sitting on a stump, breathing deeply. "Derek, where is Marlene?" asked Igor, as he reached the stump and transformed.

"Through there, Igor. They're holed up in a cabin. They fired a couple of shots, but didn't hit anything. She told me to come back and wait for you."

Igor nodded as he absorbed this information. "Why did you follow?"

"Marlene and I are immortal, you're not. I thought our chances were better against the guns, besides, I've seen her in action."

"Da."

"So, what do we do, Igor?" asked Bran.

"We give her time to deal with it. She's been getting cranky, let her feed. We'll wait here."

Even as Igor spoke they noticed Marlene returning. The Lady Hawk dropped down to transform right beside them. "Marlene's on her way back. She wasn't able to get to them."

Marlene sighed and plopped down beside them. "Those guys are dug in pretty tight there. The cabin is thick logs, the roof is turf, won't burn, the windows are small, and the door is solid wood. There's no cover to approach the door anyway. If I was alone I'd just starve them out, but ..."

"We need a diversion," sighed Igor. "Something to draw them out."

"No problem," grinned Derek. Everyone turned to give him a questioning look. "Ronni and I'll draw them out. Mount up, Lady Godiva." With that he shimmered into the stallion.

Rhonda laughed with delight and leaped to his back. As nonchalant as you please, the horse ambled out to where the men in the cabin could see the naked woman on the horse. Igor grinned and shook his head. He, Bran, and Marlene moved swiftly along the forest edge, carefully remaining out of sight.

It took a while to get the men's attention, then to lure them out. Rhonda grinned as she heard the voices from the cabin. "Sweet Jesus, there's a naked gal on a horse out there."

"What the hell are you babbling about?"

"There's a naked gal on a horse right outside the cabin."

"Right."

"There is, dammit. Get off your lazy ass and come look."

"Oh, for fuck sake. Where ... holy shit, you weren't kidding. What the hell is she doing up here in the hills with no clothes on?"

"How the hell should I know? Maybe we should ask her."

"Damn fine idea. It's getting dark out, we should invite her in to spend the night. Horse could break a leg wandering around in the dark."

"We have a plan." He slid the small window open and called out. "Hey there, Miss. Hello." She didn't appear to hear him. "Maybe she's one of them faeries or something. Maybe we shouldn't get too close."

"To hell with that," growled his companion. "I definitely plan to get closer." With that, he opened the door and stepped outside.

"Hey there, pretty lady," he called out as he approached Rhonda, who sat atop a grazing horse. "Hey, are you deaf?"

"No, but you're stupid," she replied. "Look behind you." As she spoke, she changed into a hawk and flew away.

"What the fuck???"

"Impressive, isn't she, boys?"

They spun around to see a small red-haired woman. Before they could speak, two huge wolves charged from the trees. With a yelp one man tried to raise his rifle, but he was felled from behind. The horse had kicked him.

The second man dropped his weapon in terror as he saw the woman change into a monster. He tried to scream, but it was too late. The vampire's hand gripped his throat, choking off any sound then her fangs bit deep. She drank greedily, then thrust him away.

The man crumpled to the ground, whimpering as he crawled toward his friend who lay groaning in pain. *"Both of you, be still."* Trembling in terror, both men froze in place. *"What did you steal from that motel room?"*

"Nothing."

"Why were you there?"

"Trying to confirm your ID."

"Why?"

"There's a reward. We saw it on the internet."

"Explain."

"We heard you call that man Agent Wolf. There was an Agent Wolf working with an Agent Sawchuk. There's a million dollar reward for information leading to the capture of either man. We just wanted to know if we had the right guy."

"Who put up the reward?"

"I don't know. If you find one of these guys, you contact the High Guard company. That's all we know."

Marlene looked to Igor who nodded. *"Listen carefully. You found the ID, but these were not the people you were looking for. You returned to your cabin and got drunk. You remember nothing after reaching the cabin. Now go."*

They both struggled to their feet and staggered back to the cabin. "It's nearly dark, we should be getting back," said Igor.

He morphed into the wolf and trotted away with Branimir close behind.

"So, how about it, Big Red, do I get a ride home?" asked Marlene, a twinkle in her eye. The horse shook his head and trotted away a few steps, then went back and knelt for her to mount. She leaned close and spoke in his ear. "It can be extremely dangerous to tease a vampire." He snorted, tossed his head, then trotted after the wolves.

Larise, Merle, and Peggy were watching TV in one of the rooms when the shapeshifters returned. "I couldn't figure out what they took," said Larise, as they pulled on their clothes and relaxed into chairs and on the beds.

"They didn't steal anything," replied Igor. "They were looking to confirm my ID. Apparently, I have a price on my head."

"Seriously?" asked Larise.

"Yeah, so it seems. I think I'd better report this to the king."

Harald Eldredsson sat listening to Igor's report. He'd set the phone on speaker at the mention of Terry Sawchuk's name. He looked thoughtful as Igor finished. "All right, Igor. Be careful and stay out of sight as much as possible until you get home."

"With luck we will arrive tomorrow, Sire."

"Excellent. Igor, take no chances, come straight home. The horses are already here. Give us a few minutes warning and we'll meet you at the farm."

"Will do, Sire."

"So, how's Derek doing?"

"All good now, Sire. Derek has full control of the change and has tamed the horse within."

"Good news indeed, Igor. I got the sense at one point you weren't sure if he could manage it."

"Da. Apparently, it takes longer to tame a horse than a wolf. I was getting too impatient, I guess."

Harald grinned at that. "How long does it take to tame a hawk?"

"Absolutely impossible to do, Sire," sighed Igor, a mischievous grin on his lips.

At the sounds of Rhonda's silvery laughter, Harald smiled and broke the connection. He looked up at the quiet man sitting across the table. "You heard that, Terry?"

"I did, Sire. The High Guard? They're private security, all mercs, very expensive. This doesn't sound like their type of gig at all."

"I think I'll pay a visit to their commanding officer," said Gudrun, her voice cold as deep space.

"Easy lover," said Terry, patting her hand, "we need information here, not dead bodies."

"First the one, then the other," she replied as she stood to leave, but the king's voice stopped her.

"Gudrun."

She turned back to face him, visibly fighting to gain control of the rage within her. "Yes?"

"I want to know what's going on as badly as you do. I'm not trying to stop you; I'm offering you all the resources at my disposal. Who and what do you need?"

"Just my crew, but I'll need the plane."

"Done."

"Gudrun."

She turned to the tall elegant woman who'd just spoken. "Yes, Mother?"

"I could ride along, if you don't think I'd be in the way."

"Actually, you'd be a welcome addition to the team. Let's go."

Eric had already left the great hall and had the team aboard the plane by the time Gudrun and Ella arrived. The big machine leaped into the air for the hour and a half ride to the city.

Alarms sounded throughout the building and a man raced into the plush office in the penthouse. "Sir, sir, some sort of stealth plane has landed on the roof helipad. Sir, there are armed ..." he got no further as the door to the office was swept open again.

A tall blonde woman, dressed in battle fatigues, strode through the door and pointed, the young man slunk away from her and left. "Do you know who I am?" asked the blonde, as she faced the man behind the desk.

He swallowed hard and nodded. "You're Gudrun Arielsdottir, known as the angel of death in a certain circle. It's an honor, but you didn't have to bring a strike force, I'd have been happy to meet with you. Sit down. Tell me why you've come. I assume by the fact I'm still breathing you didn't come to kill me."

"Not this time," she replied. "This time I came for information."

"Oh?"

"I have another name you might not be aware of. It's Mrs. Terry Sawchuk. I hear you've put a bounty on my husband's head. Rest assured, my friend, that does not please me. I also believe you've done this at the behest of a client. I want that client's name."

"You know better than that, Gudrun. We never disclose that kind of information." Just then, two heavily muscled men carrying assault rifles burst through the open door, but a tall woman stepped in behind them, smacked their heads together, then easily tossed the unconscious bodies aside. She winked at Gudrun, then stepped back through the door.

Gudrun gave the man a quizzical look. "You were saying?"

"No, I can't give you that information. Come on, that would be the end of my business, you know that. No one would ever trust me after that. I ..."

"Tell me what I want to know."

The man swallowed hard again, he couldn't help himself, he had to obey that voice. "Senator George Compton. It was Senator Compton who put up the reward."

"Hear me and obey. You no longer want to find Terry Sawchuk or Agent Wolf. Those men are far too dangerous. You will pull back the offer of reward, and you will stop the hunt for those men. Do you understand your instructions?"

"Yes, I understand."

"Good," said Gudrun, as she rose to her feet. "Remember how easily I took down your building and captured you. I promise you, the next time I come, you'll be dead before the sound of the alarms can reach you."

With that, she turned on her heel and marched out of the room. He went for the gun in his desk, but the tall woman was watching. She shook a finger at him and he shivered. Something about her terrified him. Instead he picked up his phone and told his secretary to cancel that offer of a reward for Terry and Igor.

The guards on the roof were still standing frozen as the plane took off. As soon as it left they returned to their posts with no memory of it having ever been there.

They were back at the Lair, reporting to the king. "Senator Compton, any relation to the former Director Compton?" asked the king.

"His father," sighed Terry. "God alone knows what Compton told his father."

"Yes, and after Gudrun's visit to the owner of High Guard Security, I expect the senator will be rather heavily guarded."

"They always are," said a hard-eyed Gudrun.

"I really don't like the idea of people poking into our affairs," mused the king. "Recommendations?"

"A quick surgical strike, Sire," said Gudrun.

"The thing of it is," sighed Terry, "how much information does the good senator already have? What does he know? Suspect? What will he do with the information? What does he really want? Who has he shared the information with?"

"All good questions, Terry, and we have no answers at all. What do you suggest?"

"Sire, I'd like to wait for Igor to get back, then have Goody put us in front of the senator, see what's really bugging his ass, get some answers to those questions."

"All right, Terry. Gudrun?"

"I'll defer to my husband on this one," she grinned. "I'm just a simple soldier, he's the super spy guy."

Harald chuckled at that. "All right, Igor should arrive tomorrow. We'll get his input once he's had a chance to catch his breath. I think that were-horse was more of a challenge than he expected."

Arrival

Igor's call came in just past noon. They'd be home in an hour or so. The king and queen took Elaine and headed for the farm. As they waited by the horse corral, Bill Walker wandered across the field to join them. Together they stood admiring the horses in the field.

"What do you think, Bill?" asked the king.

"I'll be honest, Sire, can't see much use for them myself. You got a plan?"

Harald chuckled at that. "I haven't the foggiest idea of what to do with them, but they're not my problem."

"Oh?"

"They're Derek's herd."

"So, they're his problem?"

"Precisely. Actually, Bill, some of these folks are displaced ranchers. I expect having a farmer here to help them settle in might not be a bad idea."

"That was my thought as well," agreed the old farmer. "Ah, that looks like our convoy down at the crossroads now."

Together they watched as the vehicles made their way to the old farm and pulled up near the corral. Stiffly, the riders climbed down to the ground.

"Jill." Jillian laughed and caught Elaine in her arms.

"Weren't sure we'd make it, were you?"

"I was so afraid for you. Come on, I'll introduce you to the king and queen." Elaine dragged Jill by the hand to where Harald and Sally stood smiling. "Sire, Queen Sally, this is my sister Jill. Jill, this is King Harald Eldresson, and this is Queen Sally."

"It's a pleasure to meet you, at last, Jillian," said the king, as he extended his hand to her. "Again, I must beg forgiveness for the way we first encountered each other."

If Jill was surprised at the gentleness of his handshake, she was shocked at her greeting from the queen. Sally stepped past the offered hand and hugged her tightly. "Welcome, Jill. Relax, you're safe here, and so is Derek."

Tears of relief filled Jill's eyes as she was gently released from that welcoming hug. "How did you know ...?"

"I could feel your distress the instant you got out of the truck. It's all right, Jill. You're safe here, both of you. Come on now, introduce us to your family."

Jill wiped her eyes and introduced Peggy and Merle, then Derek. The king was smiling, almost grinning, at Derek. "I'll confess, I was expecting you to be riding in that horse trailer."

Derek chuckled. "Igor finally took pity on me. I see the herd got here in one piece."

"Oh, yes. No problem at all. Aren't you going to go say hello to them?"

"Is that all right to do?" The king smiled and nodded.

"Barn door's open, you know, for a bit of privacy," said Bill. Derek nodded, then trotted to the barn and disappeared inside.

Suddenly the big red stallion burst from the barn, shot past them, soared over the fence and, with a bugling call, raced to the grazing herd in the field. Their heads came up, then there were many nose rubs, necks rubbed together as the herd welcomed the stallion.

The gathered people smiled as they watched the touching reunion. A few minutes later the stallion returned to the barn and then Derek emerged, buttoning up his shirt. "Come on inside, I'll show you guys the house," said Elaine, as she led her friends inside.

As they headed for the house, the king spoke to Igor. "Igor, it appears that the price on your head was issued by the former Director Compton's father, a senator. Terry wants Gudrun to arrange a meeting between himself, you, and the senator. What are your thoughts on this?"

"Da, I would like to speak with this man, find out what he wants, suspects, knows, and then we will know what to do about him."

"As would I, Igor. You and Ronni go home now, get some sleep. We'll talk more about this tomorrow after you've got some rest. Oh, well done on bringing Derek safely here. I think this was your toughest case yet."

Igor nodded his agreement. "Da. A big piece of the problem is, I don't understand horses. I think I like Derek. He finally got it through my head he would not subdue the horse, break him to the bridle, as he says. He was trying to win the horse's confidence, make friends with it, gain the leadership through more gentle means.

"A wolf understands strength. Kick his ass and he knows you're the alpha, he's okay with that. I guess horses are different. Anyway, once he found a way to gain control, he's been most helpful. I think he'll be a fine addition to the family."

"Thanks for that, brother wolf," grinned Derek, as he returned to bring their bags from the truck. "I have to say, Sire, that's a sweet house you set up for us. I was afraid I'd be assigned to the barn, or turned into dog food."

"We didn't dare," grinned Harald. "Elaine would have our heads. Seriously, we don't give up on our people easily, and you are one of our people, Derek. You, Jillian, and your friends are welcome here."

"Thank you. Look, I can't begin to imagine how much all this has cost you, the whole thing, sending your people to drag my sorry ass back here, providing us with a home and all."

"Now you're wondering what the catch is, what I want in return."

Derek sighed and lowered his gaze. "Yeah, that."

"Relax. For now, I want you to rest for a few days, and then we can discuss the rest."

"The rest?"

"We're a small people, Derek. There are only a few of us and our allies. We all have to find a way to contribute to the greater good, to keeping the race of non-humans safe, to help ensure our continued survival.

"There's no hurry, but we'll find a way for you and yours to contribute."

"I could use a hand on the farm," grinned Bill.

"Sure, but the first time I see you holding a bridle and looking at a wagon, all bets are off."

"Dang," grinned Bill, as he slapped Derek on the shoulder and turned away. "He'll do, Sire. He'll do." As he walked away, Bill spoke to a strange creature that was approaching. "Hi, Tanya."

"Hi, Farmer Bill. Want some help with the chickens?"

"You keep your paws off my chickens, young lady."

The creature giggled and approached the group. "What the hell is that?" she heard Derek ask as she approached. "I'm a witch-what-who, what the hell are you?"

With a rueful chuckle and a shake of his head, Derek sank to a cross-legged position on the ground. "Fair question. Hi, I'm Derek, a were-horse. So, what the heck is a witch-what-who?"

He held out his hand and she put her paw into it. "Hi, I'm Tanya, a multi animal. Igor calls me a forest witch who can turn into different animals but doesn't know what one she likes best."

"More than one? Cool, so can you do completely human?"

"I can, but that body was broken, it hurts too much. This one is more fun. So, horseman, take me for a ride some day?"

"Sure. No saddle though. I'm a wild horse, no saddles."

"It's okay, I'll grow claws, so I can hang on. Are the girls in the house?"

"Yes, they're inside," smiled Harald. "You go on in, Tanya, introduce yourself."

Derek rose easily to his feet as she scampered off toward the house. "She's cute, I like her."

"She's a bundle of mischief and fun all right," said Igor.

"So, not everybody here is a hard-nosed super secret agent?"

"No," replied Harald. "Not everybody is able to fill that role. Those of us who can make sure they're safe to be themselves."

"I find that reassuring," said Derek. "Are there others like Tanya?"

"Some. Actually, Tanya is far more functional that some."

Derek looked thoughtful for a moment. "Okay, I expect I'll fall somewhere between Tanya and Igor on the useful scale. I'm in. I'll do whatever I can to help the cause."

"Actually, Sire, I think Derek could make a useful agent."

"Oh?"

Igor was grinning. "Da. I was ready to skin him when he and Marlene raced past us, but it was Derek's idea for he and Ronni to do the Lady Godiva thing to pull those guys out of their hideout. The man's a thinker, not a warrior."

Harald chuckled at that. "Thinkers can be useful on a mission. Maybe this fellow can help you develop more patience, Igor."

"Da. If I don't go mad first. With your permission, Sire, I'll head for home. I need to check in with the pack, then sleep for a week."

"Get some rest, Igor. We'll take a look at the Compton thing tomorrow, decide what's to be done there."

Senator Compton

It was midafternoon the next day, and they were gathered in the great hall. Gudrun was fussing, Terry was lost in thought, and Igor was dozing in his chair. Harald grinned as Tanya entered with Derek in tow. "Found him hanging out with the herd, Sire," she grinned.

"Thank you, Tanya," smiled Harald.

Tanya poked Igor in the ribs. "Wake up, the king's talking." She shrieked with laughter as he made a grab for her and missed. She scampered out the door, still laughing. Igor grinned as he watched her go.

Harald introduced Derek to those assembled then got down to business. "All right, we're all here, let's get to it. Terry."

"Thank you, Sire," said the powerfully built man, as he rose to his feet. "All right, folks, we have a problem. "A year ago, the director of a secret government agency met his fate at our hands. That man and I had issues and he'd set himself to make an end of me no matter what it took. Now, his father, a senator has put a bounty on my head; mine and Igor's.

"Gudrun has convinced the security company to recall the bounty and to stop any further search for the two of us.

168

However, that still leaves us vulnerable. How much does the senator know, what does he suspect, who has he confided in, what other steps has he taken?

"It won't be enough to just assassinate him. We need answers to those questions. We need to find and erase any and all evidence he may have in his possession, anything he may have shared with others. The first question we need to answer is: how do we proceed from this point?

"Okay folks, we're open for ideas. Let's hear 'em."

Gudrun stopped her pacing and sat beside Terry. "Personally, I'd like to grab him, drag his sorry ass back here for a serious grilling."

"Back here?" asked the king. "Why here?"

"Here, there, doesn't really matter. We just need to get him somewhere far away from his comfort zone, some place where we can speak freely without fear of interference. I said here because this man could be the worst danger we've faced so far.

"Everyone in this room has a stake in this, we all look at the world differently and therefore could have different questions for him, questions that could reveal more than a single person might discover."

"I know just the place," said Terry. "Let's take him to the building where his son interrogated me."

"Oh yeah," grinned Gudrun. "Sounds perfect to me."

"Then we have a plan," said the king. "Tommy, locate our man for Gudrun."

"Already got him, Sire. He's on holiday on his ranch. Sending the coordinates to Gudrun's phone now."

"Tommy, you're the best. Gudrun, take whoever you need, bring that man to the location you spoke of."

"I'll take my crew, Sire. Terry, you stay with Harald.

"Yes, dear." He grinned as he watched his wife walk away, signaling to her men.

"Igor, can I borrow Bran and Larise?" asked Gudrun. Igor nodded and the two agents rose and followed Gudrun out.

The king turned in his seat and shrugged his shoulders. "Now for my team, I'll want Ella, Terry, Igor, Rhonda, Derek, and Sally with me."

"Me?" exclaimed Derek. "Why me?"

"Because you need to see this up close and personal. Gudrun will be using the plane, looks like we'll be riding the bus. We leave in one hour. Torvil, the Lair is yours, make sure I have a home to come back to."

Just then Terry's phone buzzed, and he glanced at it. "Not to worry, Sire. Gudrun says to sit tight, she'll send Eric with the plane once she has the target in hand."

Harald grinned and nodded.

Senator Jack Compton paced around his spacious living room, drink in hand. His wife sighed and looked away, nursing her own drink. "Sir," said the young aide, who watched the senator closely, "perhaps you should ..."

"Fuck you, Dylan. Don't you fucking dare tell me to stop drinking. Sweet Jesus, I spent a fortune on those assholes and suddenly they turn chickenshit. Why? Who got to them? How? How could anyone get to those people and scare the shit out of them? Good god, I didn't think anything could scare Thurston Brady."

"Sir ..."

"No, Sawchuk got to them somehow. How the hell does he do it?"

"Sir, are you so certain Agent Sawchuk got to them? How could he? What could he possibly have on a man like Thurston Brady? What could he do that would scare a man like him?"

"I have no idea at all, but we'll soon find out. I've asked Brady here tonight. I want answers and he'd damn well better provide ... there he is now." There was the sound of a car outside, then Thurston's voice. The security guard let him then it all went to hell in a hurry.

There were shots fired as Thurston entered, and he was suddenly thrust into the room. The woman screamed as Thurston went for his gun, but he was cut down. Three people in military gear, wearing masks burst into the room. The woman who led them shot Thurston Brady through the heart. "I told you to back off."

She turned to the senator, grabbed him by the collar and thrust him towards the two men. "Take him." She then turned to where the woman and young aide huddled together. She spoke in a voice from a distant hell. *"Stand up. Go to another room and have sex. You were not here when the shots were fired. You returned from your tryst to find men dead and the senator missing. Go."*

They followed her instructions, trembling in fear. Gudrun turned to see Jimmy arching an eyebrow at her. "Have sex?"

"They're already lovers, couldn't you tell?"

"No."

"We burst into the room, shot a man, and grabbed the senator. She didn't run to the senator, she ran to his aide who got between me and her. Lovers. Let's go." A moment later a car sped across the yard and out onto the plains. A strange looking plane was hidden there, and the senator was herded onboard, a bag dropped over his head, and his hands and feet secured.

Trembling in fear, the senator felt the plane rise into the air, then a while later it descended. His feet were cut loose, and he was herded into a car, driven somewhere then hustled into a building. He cursed and fought as he was stripped naked and tied to a chair. The bag was removed from his head.

He fought to let his eyes adjust to the harsh lights. Finally his vision cleared. He was in the middle of an empty room, a warehouse probably. His captor, the woman, was there with him, he assumed the rest were standing guard. He was right.

"Who are you people? What do you want? Do you have any idea how much trouble you're in? I'm a United States Senator, for Christ's sake." Her only response was laughter. Try as hard as he could, she wouldn't answer him, all he could do was sit there, shivering in the cold, and silently pray.

Terry glanced at his phone. "Saddle up, folks, Gudrun's got her man and Eric's on his way to pick us up." They assembled at the hangar, all in the military uniform of Gudrun's crew. Each had a mask in their pocket.

"Wow, now that's a hard looking crew," grinned Eric, as he opened the doors for them.

Sally laughed and poked him in the ribs. "Shut up, Eric." They settled into seats and the plane lifted off.

Harald moved forward and settled into the co-pilot's seat. "Report," he said softly.

"Sweet and easy, Sire. We landed at the ranch, back out of sight of the house. We approached the house and took down the guards just as the head guy for High Guard Security showed up. Gudrun plugged him and we grabbed the senator."

"There's no trace of your presence there?"

"Just the dead guards and the High Guard guy."

"Eric."

"It's how we work, Sire. We strike hard and fast, no witnesses. After we're done with the senator, you can let him go and he can tell a story about kidnappers being paid off by his wife, or we can pop him and tell a different story."

Harald sighed and relaxed back in the seat. "Sorry, Eric. It was done right, exactly how I'd have done it in the old days. I guess I'm getting a bit paranoid in this age of intrusive electronics."

"I get that, Sire. Actually, I think Gudrun has a plan to throw suspicion on the Russian mob."

"I like that, perhaps I'll speak to him in Russian first, just to add some weight to it." He rose and returned to the main seating area. "Eric tells me Gudrun wants to throw the suspicion onto the Russian mob. So, we'll confer among ourselves in Russian where he can hear us, then we'll question him in English. It'll make the compulsion stronger when we give him the idea that it was the Russians who kidnapped him."

There were chuckles all round at that. A while later the plane landed in a parking lot beside a warehouse building. Jimmy and Vassily were on exterior guard, and they swiftly pulled the tarp over the plane. Eric led them inside, past where Larise and Bran were on guard, and into the interrogation room.

The senator swallowed hard as two men pulled chairs up close to him and pulled off the masks. "Who the hell are you people?" Igor responded in Russian. "What the hell did he just say?"

Terry chuckled. "It wasn't polite. So, Senator Compton, I hear you're looking for me. Care to tell me why?"

"Who the fuck are you?"

"Terry Sawchuk."

"You."

"Me. So, why are you looking for me?"

"I want to put you away forever, you fucking traitor."

"Heavy accusation. Got any proof of that?"

"Plenty, more than enough to have you shot as a traitor, you and the rest of those freaks."

"Freaks?" asked another voice as a huge man stepped towards him.

The senator visibly flinched. He swallowed hard as a woman put a hand on the big man's arm and he stepped back. "Look, you people are in it deep here. Your only chance is to let me go. I'll give you a twenty-four-hour head start, time enough to get out of the country."

"Explain what you mean by the word freaks," demanded another voice.

"You know damn well what I mean. Oh, you thought you were so damned smart in New York when you killed my boy, but my son was smarter. He got you, and he got evidence. We saw film of that woman, or whatever the hell she is. He knew that freak would come for him, so he always wore a micro cam and a wire."

The senator began to laugh hysterically. "Search all you want; you'll never find it. You and the rest of those freaks are all going to die. I've got a full file on you, Sawchuk, you and your freaks. If I don't send the password in less than two hours that file will go to every department ..."

"Be silent." Gudrun stepped forward. *"This is your phone. Send the password, and only the password, now."* Swift strokes of a knife released his hands. Trembling with fear, he sent the coded message. *"You will now answer all questions truthfully and fully."*

Another man stepped forward; it was Tommy. "Have you shared your file with anyone?"

"No."

"Why not?" asked Igor.

"I wasn't ready. We needed more evidence."

"Where is that file and back-ups kept?" asked Tommy.

"It's in a secret place in the tack room of the horse barn. The back-up is in the cloud storage."

"Can you access the back-up with your phone?"

"Yes."

"Delete it."

The senator didn't move a muscle. *"Do as he bid you,"* said that terrible voice.

The senator used his phone to access his cloud storage account and deleted the file, Tommy watching closely over his shoulder. "Delete all of it, everything in that account," said Tommy. The senator complied.

"Where else do you have files that pertain to us?"

"My computer at home and on my office computer."

"Tommy, can you ...?"

"Working, Sire. Senator, I've just sent an e-mail to your phone. Open it and forward it to your home computer and your office computer." The senator complied. "That will do it, Sire. That was a virus I designed myself. Now all we need is what he's got hidden in that horse barn."

"That place will be crawling with security and police now," said Eric. "We could bomb the barn, but ..."

"I can get in there unseen," said Derek. "It's a horse barn, right?"

"I'll go with you, be the lookout." Said Rhonda.

"Gudrun, can you get them close enough?" asked the king.

"We can, but it's nearly daylight. We should get out of here and wait for darkness."

"To the plane then. Bring him."

A bag was dropped over the senator's head and he was carried to the plane and tossed aboard. The plane rose swiftly then shot away. There was a thunderous crack as it broke the sound barrier.

Off World

A while later the plane settled down, and they filed off. "Get some sleep, people," said the king. "Throw the senator into a cell."

"Shouldn't we feed him first?" asked Derek.

"No," replied the king. "Let him stew in his own juice until we awaken. We'll feed him then. For now he gets a cold cell and time to reflect."

Derek watched the king and queen walk away, a puzzled expression on his face. "Come on," said Igor. "Watch now."

They watched as Eric pushed the senator into a cell then locked the door. The man was still shouting and cursing as they all walked away. Once out of sight the king signaled Tanya to approach. He spoke to the girl for a moment and they saw the look of gleeful mischief cross her face as she nodded.

Seeing the look on Derek's face the king relented. "Derek, I wanted you with us tonight so you would see first hand what we're up against, how vital it is to keep out of the public eye."

"Yeah, I knew what would likely happen if anybody ever saw me, but listening to him call us freaks, see the hate in his eyes, that drove the lesson home all right. Can I ask why you said not to give him food?"

"That man is now where he wants to put Terry and Igor, in a cold dark cell, naked, without food or water. He will get both food and water, but only if he can make friends with a freak. Tanya will make sure he has what he needs, but he'll have to earn it. His food, his continued existence will be possible only through the kindness of a creature he reviles. She'll mess with his mind while she does it though."

Derek chuckled at that. "Now that's poetic justice. I like it. So, am I going after that computer stuff tonight?"

"You are," replied the king. "Get some rest and be back here before dark." Derek nodded and started away.

"Derek, I'll give you a lift," said Igor. "Come."

They climbed into a jeep and Igor drove to the house where Jill and company were waiting. "Igor ..."

"I know. You will go in alone tonight, the Lady Hawk being the lookout for you. I'm not jealous, Derek. Just make sure I never have a reason to be."

His grin of mischief gave it away and Derek chuckled. "Understood. Igor, thanks for not giving up on me."

Igor nodded. "Go on, your woman is waiting." Derek got out and Igor drove back to the castle. As he entered the mansion he saw Tanya going with a water bottle and a package of sandwiches. He gave her a wink and she giggled as she headed for the cells below.

Tanya placed the water and food a short distance from the senator's cell. She then approached and, rising up on her back paws, peered into his cell. "What the fuck are you looking at, freak?"

"Aren't you cold? You don't have any fur."

"No I don't have any fur, and yes I'm cold. Bugger off."

"Hey, there's no need to be nasty. You're never getting out of there anyway, so screw you too, you furless wonder. Nobody ever gets out once the door closes." Fighting a giggle, she lowered herself out of his sight.

"Up yours. Wait. Hey, freak, or whatever you are. Come back."

Grinning from ear to ear, Tanya replied. "Why should I? You're mean, just like the last guy who died in there."

"Wait, last guy who died in here? Men have died in here?"

"Yup. You piss off the king, you go in the cell, and then you die. No food, no water. Humans don't survive long that way."

"Let me out, come on, you can do it. No one would ever know. Come on, you can't just let me die in here."

"Are you crazy? I'd be skinned alive if I let you out, besides what would be the point?"

"The point? We could get away. At least we'd have a chance. I could get to a phone, call for help, get us both out of here. Come on, you can do it, I know you can."

"A phone? Call for help? Where do you think we are? Good grief, human, there's no phones on this planet. Even if there were, there's nobody within three light years for you to call."

"What? What the hell are you talking about, planet?"

"You were brought in on the ship. You're not on Earth anymore, moron. Geez. Look, maybe I can get you some water, but I can't promise."

Tanya scooted away and around the corner. Up in the great hall the king and queen were laughing. "That girl has such a wild imagination," grinned Harald.

"Oh yeah," smiled Sally. "She'll mess with his mind."

Down by the cells Tanya passed the senator a bottle of water and the sandwiches. He ate greedily and drank all the water. "Thanks kid, now about how we get out of here."

"Look, I told you, I can't let you out, and there's nowhere for you to go if I did. We're on a different planet, nothing outside those walls but a few trees and an endless desert. There are only two outposts on this planet, nowhere to go."

"Kid, that's pure bullshit."

"If you say so," she replied, as she started away. "Good luck with your new job."

"Hey, wait. Come back. What do you mean, my new job?"

Tanya grinned up at him. "Did you enjoy the food?"

"Yeah, wait, there was something in the food. You little freak, what did you do to me?"

"There was an organic control trigger in it. You're all ours now."

"What the hell is an organic control trigger?"

"It's organic, can't be detected by your people. Your tech isn't advanced enough. What does it do? By now it's made its way to, and attached itself to, your brain, no way to detect it, no way to get it out. The king will probably send you back to gather more information about Earth's defenses. Well, if you're lucky he will. If not, you'll die in there like the last guy. Bye!"

"Hey, wait. Kid, come back. Come back here you goddamn freak."

Giggling, Tanya hid around the corner and listened to him swear and plead for a while then she went up to the great hall to report to the king.

"Tanya, that was amazing," grinned Harald, as she entered the great hall.

"Thanks," she replied shyly. "So, are we going to up the game on him a bit?"

"Up the game? What do you mean?"

"Well, he's seen me, but has he seen a vampire?"

"He's seen Gudrun on his son's film, but we're trying to destroy that before it gets out. Why?"

"I've got an idea. If Miss Marlene and Victor will help me, I think we can cinch it."

"What's going through that devious mind of yours, Little Sister?" asked Victor.

"Okay, you and Marlene get into uniform, then go full vampire. You use harsh voices as you walk past his cell, talking about the coming invasion of Earth, how you can't wait to get at it. Stuff like that."

The senator suddenly heard something outside his cell. He looked out the small barred window and saw two creatures in uniform. They were like the one who killed his son. He listened to them talking, a deep fear gnawing at him.

"Why are you using that hideous language?"

"We must practice if we are to fool their defenses."

"Of course, do you think the invasion will come soon?"

"I do. It can't come soon enough for me. I've had a few tastes of those human creatures, I want more."

"Patience, my brother-in-arms, patience. Soon you will have all you want."

They slowly walked away, out of his hearing, then returned to the great hall. "Well, how was that?"

"Perfect, Marlene," chuckled the king. "I'll add a compulsion to seal it before we put him back on the plane tonight. Once Derek and Rhonda give the all-clear, we'll let him loose.

"Tommy, how's that bank thing coming?"

"All done, Sire. I've extracted five million from the senator's accounts and made it look like he did it. I transferred the money a few times, anyone trying to track it will lose the trail in Russia."

"But that's not where it is?"

"No, Sire," grinned Tommy, "it's in your account in Germany, in case we ever need to retreat there."

"Excellent. All right, people, get some rest."

Homeward Bound

It was late afternoon when the king called them together at the hangar. "So, are we ready? Does everyone know what to do?"

"Yes, Sire," replied Derek. "Gudrun gets us as near as possible with the plane then I go in as Big Red. I locate the tack room, find and destroy all the evidence hidden there, and then set the tack room on fire. Ronni will be my lookout."

"Once Derek gives the all-clear, I put the compulsion on the senator, and then let him go," grinned Gudrun. "He tells everybody about the alien abduction, but all the evidence points to a kidnapping. He paid the ransom and was set free."

"Good luck, people. Igor, you're not going with them?"

"I have no job in this mission, I'm going back to bed."

Rhonda stepped close and put her hand over his heart. "What's going on here?"

He sighed and hugged her gently. "On our last mission things were misinterpreted, misunderstandings occurred, and things nearly went badly for the wrong reasons, my pretty bird. I love you, I like Derek, and this will

186

demonstrate that I trust you, both of you. Go, do what you do best, make me proud."

"No, Igor, there's no need ..."

"Go, you're wasting time."

"I'm not going anywhere, not with this the way it is. We're a team, you and I, my lover. We work together or not at all. I like Derek too, but he's not you, and I'm not going on any mission without you. Now get your furry ass on that plane."

"You have your orders, Igor," chuckled the king.

"The wolf gets no respect," grumbled Igor, as he climbed aboard the plane. "What's the point of being the alpha if all I do is take orders?"

"Oh don't whine," giggled Rhonda, as she snuggled tight against him.

"Ronni, this is not necessary. I trust you and Derek to behave properly. I ..."

"Hush now, my darling boy, this has nothing to do with Derek. This is about us. Igor, I learned something really important on our mission out west. I learned that I get caught up in the job and lose sight of what's most important of all.

"Igor, our time together is finite, we both know and accept that. However, I can see where I took certain things for granted. Never again. I'll have only so much time with you, then I'll have to let you go.

"Until that day arrives, I'll spend every moment possible in your company, drag ever drop of joy from each moment I have with you. You're not here because of the thing out west, you're here for me, because I won't go without you."

"Sweet Ronni, one day you will have to."

"I know, but it's not this day. Today, I get to keep you with me. Oh, in case you're wondering, you're not allowed to go on a mission without me either. Just saying."

He chuckled and pulled her closer. "I wouldn't dream of it, my pretty bird."

Just then they heard the senator being brought out. "Be silent, human." With the black bag over his head and his arms in restraints, the senator was stuffed aboard the plane. Eric signaled that it would be a fast take off, so everybody buckled in.

The plane leaped into the air then streaked away. With a grunt the senator fell to the floor as the g-forces hit him. Grinning, Igor hauled him back into a seat. No one spoke during the flight, and the senator was getting nervous. Finally, he felt the plane land.

"You know what to do," said Gudrun, as she hauled the senator from the plane and released his hands and pulled the bag off his head. His jaw dropped as a man changed into a horse and a woman leaped in the air and flew away as a hawk. Another man changed into a wolf and followed the horse until he saw the barn in the distance then dropped to the ground.

Igor settled himself on the hillock, in clear view of the barn. He would be ready if needed, but this was Derek and Ronni's task. He would leave them to it.

Derek ran easily, not wanting to draw too much attention. He slowed to an easy trot as he neared the barn, then dropped to a walk as he reached the big open doors. The hawk swept inside and perched in the rafters.

The tack room was easy enough to find. A quick look around showed him the coast was clear, so he morphed back into the man and slipped inside. A moment later he found the hidden panel and slid it aside. The small safe was there and he quickly tapped out the combination.

The door opened easily to his touch. He retrieved the memory stick from the safe, then gathered some rags, dumped some oil on them. Grinning, he found the lighter right where he expected to find it, in a box beside the portable forge and anvil. A moment later he had a fire going in the rags.

"Incoming," said a woman's voice. Derek slipped out of the tack room and tossed the memory stick into the air. The hawk caught it in her talons and flew away. He transformed into the horse and screamed a warning then bolted from the barn.

As he ran he heard the cry of "Fire!" behind him. That would keep the humans on the ranch busy. He broke into a gallop as the hawk flew on ahead. Derek arrived to find Rhonda already dressed and cuddled into Igor's arms.

As he shimmered back into the man and began pulling on his clothes, Gudrun grabbed the senator. *"You were abducted by aliens, they plan to invade Earth, they cannot be stopped. You will never try to locate or gather information about us again, but will just accept the coming fate. Go now, return to your people."*

They watched as the naked man stumbled away towards the ranch hidden behind the low hill. As soon as he was out of sight the plane took off and returned to the Lair. "Well. How did it go?" asked the king, as they debarked from the plane.

"Smooth as silk," grinned Gudrun. "As soon as the two infiltrators got back I put the compulsion on the senator and sent him home. He probably babbling to someone now about the aliens. Ronni?"

"Easy money for me," she replied. "I flew in, watched for guards while Derek did his thing. He tossed me the data stick and I flew back with it." She passed the info stick to the king who passed it off to Tommy. "Derek?"

"Oh, I went in slow, so I wouldn't arouse suspicion. The coast was clear, so I changed and entered the tack room. The safe was where he said, the combination worked, and the stick was all there was in it. I found some oil and rags, the portable forge and lighter for the gas, set the fire, then we beat feet back to the plane."

"Igor?"

"Me? Sire, you saw. I had no job there. Hawk and horse headed out, I went wolf and caught a nap until they got back."

"You didn't supervise?"

"What supervise, they knew what to do, I didn't. What do I know of barns and tack rooms? Derek knows these things. He knew what to look for, how to start the fire."

The king grinned and gave Igor's shoulder a friendly squeeze. "So you watched nervously from a distance, ready to leap in at the first sign of trouble."

Igor sighed and chuckled. "Da, that."

"Get some rest, people. Gudrun, are we done with this now?"

"Yes, Sire. I'd say we're free of that one now. Tanya's idea was awesome. He'll never tell a soul what he's seen, but he'll spend the rest of his days looking at the sky. We're off the hook from that quarter."

"Good to know. Igor, your final assessment of Derek and his people."

"I trust him, Sire, and I believe he's fully aware now. I believe your plan for them is a good one."

"Plan for them?" asked Derek.

"Soon, my friend," said the king as he walked away. "Soon."

Two weeks later the king was leaning against the horse corral, chatting with Derek, Jillian, Peggy, and Merle. Harald gazed at the horses and smiled. "What do you think we should do with them, Derek? They still seem pretty wild to me."

"They are, Sire. If it were up to mem I'd put them back where they came from."

"Getting the old itch to run with the herd?"

Derek laughed at that. "No, Sire. Don't get me wrong, I'd love nothing more than to race the wind across the plains, but Big Red's days of leading this herd are over. That young palomino there has taken over by the looks of things."

Harald smiled and turned to Jillian. "I have to say, Jillian, you disappoint me."

"Sire?" Her eyes flew wide with fear, then she saw the mischievous grin on his face. "All right, tell me how I disappoint."

"By Elaine's estimation, you should have driven me near to madness by now, trying to convince me to let you move back to that ranch out west, but you've never said a word."

"Sorry to disappoint," she grinned. "Actually, when I believed that was the best place for Derek, I was hell bent on that plan. I didn't know you or these people, and as you may know, I have a few trust issues."

Harald chuckled at that. "So tell me, Jill, best case scenario, what would you rather do, stay here, or go back to your old life?"

"Given the choice? I'd go back in a heartbeat. Yes, this place you made for us is awesome, and having the chance to reconnect with Elaine has been pure gold, but ... you know ..."

"What about you folks? Peggy, Merle?"

They looked at each other then smiled. "Jill said it best. This place is great, but ..."

"It's not home?"

"Yeah, that," said Merle.

"People, I've gone to a lot of trouble to create a safe haven here for non-humans and their people. However, not everybody lives here. Gina and Marco are in New York, Peter has returned to Russia with a pack of werewolves, others have taken up residence in Germany. The point is, as long as I can trust you to stay out of the public eye and know I can call on you at any time, I have no reason to keep you here if you'd rather be elsewhere."

"Are you serious?"

"Yes, I am, Jill. I know that ranch was in a bit of trouble financially, so I bought it. It needs work and I'd like to put a crew of caretakers in there. Would you folks be interested in that?"

"My god, are you serious?"

"Yes, Jill, I think he is," grinned Derek.

Harald passed Merle an envelope. "That's the deed to your ranch, Merle. I'll need you to provide a safe place for my horse to hide out. There's been a bank account set up in the name of the ranch. Tommy will see you have access to it.

"Derek, I've decided to set these horses free, so I'll need you to make sure they get back to where they came from. Tommy will set everything up for you from here, but you'll have to greet them on the other side when they get off the train.

"After that I'll need you to be my eyes and ears out west. You'll be my agent out there, watching for any other non-humans that may crop up, helping my other agents as needed. Does this work for you?"

"You know it does, Sire. I ..."

"None of that now. You're an agent of the vampire king. Jillian, your task will be to keep me up to date on things as necessary. You can relay the mundane things through Elaine and contact me directly in case of an emergency.

"I understand you folks would rather go home. I get that. Also, this Lair has limited space available. We still have lots of room, but I like the idea of having agents spread around the country.

"Start packing, people, Elaine will be here soon with your travel arrangements." With that, the king climbed back into the jeep and returned to the castle.

Derek went with the driver to get the horses onto a rail car, then took a cab to the airport. They had to fly commercial as the stealth plane was on its way to Europe on another assignment. Igor and Rhonda were there with Elaine to see them off. By the day's end they were all back in the old ranch house.

A week later Derek and Jill sat beside the road and watched the wild horses grazing. "Feeling like you want to join them?" she teased.

He chuckled at that. "No girl, but I know what I'd like to do."

"Tell me."

"There's nobody around anywhere. I'd like to shift, get you on my back, then see if I can outrun the wind. Just head out onto that prairie and give it all I've got. Whaddya say, want to race the wind with me?"

"Let's go, Stud," she grinned as she stood and pulled her hat on tight. Suddenly the big red stallion was beside her. She leaped to his back as he exploded away from the old truck. Jillian shrieked with delight as she leaned over his neck and clung tightly to his mane as he thundered across the open plain.

King Harald lay back against the pillows and pulled Sally down onto his shoulder. "Sally, my love."

"Yes, dear?"

"Remember when you said you'd look far into the future for a hint of what was to come?"

"Yes."

"What did you see? You've never spoken a word about it."

Sally was quiet for several moments, then spoke softly. "I got the sense that what I saw was thousands of years in the future. I saw Rhonda, standing at the edge of a cliff. She had a cloak about her shoulders, a gold circlet on her head, and a weapon of some sort in her hand.

"Gudrun stood at her side, in full vampire mode, Victor on the other, both fully armed, and the tigress at her feet. Her eyes were hard as stone. As Rhonda turned I could see them, wolves, hundreds, maybe thousands of them. As she faced them they shifted to human form and knelt, one fist raised in the air. They all shouted, "Hail to the Queen!

"One approached, the alpha I'd guess, and knelt before her. He looked a lot like Branimir. "They're coming, my Queen," he said. "The human army is nearly here."

"That's all I saw. Harald, the future's not set in stone. The fact that Ronni and Igor sorted themselves out changes that future. Still, it frightened me."

"Go to sleep now, my lady love. As you say, that future will not come to pass now." Even though he knew that possible future had been avoided, Harald now knew the power of the

Lady Hawk's personality could thrust her into a leadership role. He silently vowed to mentor her at every opportunity.

The End

Author's note: The queen's vision is all too accurate, as we will soon see. Stay with me now as we ...

Heir to the Throne

by

Prudence MacLeod

After the destruction

The carnage had been beyond description, beyond belief, beyond imagining. The three vampires kicked in the door of the church, bringing a madness, a hell, none of the people could have imagined. Two of the beasts tore into the gathered families, ripping and tearing at them. Blood and bodies were everywhere.

Those who tried to escape were seized by the third vampire and tossed back into the room to be killed and fed on by the others. The scar-faced man laughed in mad delight as his creations mangled and destroyed the gathered people there, their tortured screams music to his ears.

When it was done, or it seemed to be so, he attacked and killed the other two vampires. "There is only one god," he said, "and I am that one true god." He tore the heads from the vampires and threw them out the window, then set fire to the church.

As the flames leaped up, a small boy who'd hidden under the altar, noticed movement. One man was still alive. Terrified, the boy nonetheless went to him and dragged him out from under the bodies. "That way," gasped the man as he tried to point. The child understood and together they made their way out of the burning building. The mad vampire was gone.

Darkness had fallen before the boy managed to get the injured man to his home. Only then did the child break down and weep, crying out his anguish for his mother and father, his sisters, all of whom had died in the attack.

201

While the boy wept, the man struggled to bind his own wounds. He had also lost his family in that church of blood, his wife and son tortured and killed before his eyes. As the boy wept and cried pitifully for his mother, Melosh bandaged his own wounds and, pushing down his grief and sorrow, vowed vengeance. He would find a way to kill the demons, and then he would hunt them.

Returning to the boy, he took him into his arms to comfort him. "Hush now. You are Johan, yes? We will learn, study together, and we will hunt them, you and I, Johan. We will hunt and destroy the beasts, torture them as they tortured our families, then kill them, destroy them utterly. For now, we must leave this place. I know where to go, where we can hide, learn, and grow strong, you and I."

He carried the child outside and tucked him into his old car. This village was no longer safe. Two days later they arrived at a rundown cottage that had once been the gate house for a nobleman's mansion. The Bolsheviks had burned the manor house long ago, but the cottage remained.

THE FIRST DAYS AT THE cottage were difficult for Melosh. Even though he and his wife had three children, he had taken little interest in their care. Now he had to care for the child that had saved him from the fire, and he had no idea what to do for him. Both man and boy were numbed by what had happened, what they'd suffered, what they'd witnessed.

The place was damp and moldy after several years of being uninhabited. As they struggled to clean it and make it more livable, they found several of the old man's books. The most dog-eared volume was called The Vampire Hunter. Holding it in his hand as though a priceless treasure, Melosh gazed at the faded cover for a long time, then he set it aside. He planned to study it in detail later.

Melosh's grandfather had lived in that cottage for many years, and often spoke of the wealth his master had buried before the Bolsheviks had come. It took Melosh and Johan eight years to find it, but find it they did. That gave them the financial means to continue the vendetta, the hunt for vampires.

They studied books, combat arts, weapons, medieval torture methods, plus any and all monster lore they could find. The boy grew into a man, a man with a burning rage inside, a deep desire to avenge his mother, and a silent, secret, hatred for Melosh, the man who forced him to remember, the man who would not let him forget his mother's screams. Melosh fed that rage in him, nurtured it, drove it, for it matched his own.

He would often find the boy outside, gazing up at the night sky. "Johan?"

"Mother used to love looking at the stars. She would catch me watching her when I was supposed to be sleeping, and she would quietly call me out beside her. I'd crawl up into her lap and star gaze with her. I sometimes come out here and look at the stars to remember."

"Yes, remember, but remember the last moments of her life, Johan. Never forget that. No mother is safe while that thing lives. Remember that. We must find and kill it. Remember her screams."

The boy, nearly a man now, turned and grabbed the older man by the collar, shaking him. "You think I don't remember? You think I don't hear her screams, feel her terror, see her step between me and the monster? Every moment of every day, I hear those screams."

He thrust the older man away. "Sometimes I just want to remember her gentleness, her smile, the touch of her hand. Tell me you don't feel the same for your wife."

"I do, Johan, I do. She, too, enjoyed the stars on a summer's night. That is why I'm so determined to kill this thing, to make the night safe for all mothers and wives to enjoy."

"We will avenge them, Melosh. We will slay that monster and then they can rest peacefully. On that day I will join my mother in that world beyond."

"You mean heaven? You would kill yourself?"

"Da. This is no life, Melosh. Heaven? I don't believe in that place, only hell. I believe in that one because I've been there. No, we will kill the monsters, then leave this world to the people. This is no place for monsters."

"So, you think we're monsters now?"

"Are we not? After what we've done, after what we plan to do? What else have we become?" With that the young man stood and went back inside, to his bed, to blessed sleep, the only place he could find relief from the bloody images in his mind, and he hated Melosh for constantly reminding him.

Up to that point they had only hunted and captured animals, large animals, bears, elk, and tortured them as they learned and practiced how to confine and control large powerful creatures. The next day they planned to hunt a man, a man who had beaten his wife to death, a man the entire small town hated and feared.

They found him and took him down with tranquilizer darts, just as they'd practiced. The man awakened slowly as the drug wore off. Suddenly terrified, he began to struggle, but his movements cause incredible pain, so he lay still whimpering. A young man approached, and he tried to plead with him, but a large ball gag in his mouth prevented speech.

"You are awake now, I see. Do not struggle, for the wire will cause you great pain. Ah, what does it matter, I will cause you great pain anyway." He grabbed the wire that confined the man and twisted it tighter, eliciting a scream.

"Hurts, doesn't it? It might interest you to know I sat outside your house listening to your wife scream, twice. Sadly, I was not there to prevent her death." He bent closer to stare into the man's eyes. "There is no one here to prevent your death at my hands either. Just as your wife saw her death in your eyes, now you see your own death in mine." The captive screamed again as the wire was tightened once more, then the young man walked away.

They stood together as they finished burying the man's body. The younger man was quiet, gazing at the fresh dirt. "It was only just that he die, Johan, pay for his crime, his brutality against the weak."

"I know, but was it necessary to torture him?"

"It was a learning experience. As he paid for his cruelty, he helped us in our holy quest, taught us how to bring the screams from the vampire when we catch him. At the end, he finally did something good for his fellow man."

"Holy quest, Melosh? Holy? No, there is nothing holy about what we do, what we have become."

"We do what we must so the rest of the people will not know what we know, will not suffer as we suffered. We do what we must to learn the things we need to know, so we can protect the weak."

"Protect the weak? Is that why we do what we do, truly?"

"That is part of it, yes, but we do it to bring justice as well. That and we are preparing ourselves for the ultimate battle. Johan, you know what we will face. Save your pity for those who deserve it, not scum like this one was, or monsters like the vampire. Scum like this one will serve our needs as we learn what we need to know for the final battle with the beast."

Johan just nodded then took up his shovel and walked back toward the car. Melosh clapped a gentle hand on his shoulder. "Tomorrow we leave this place. We will go to St. Petersburg, find a place to work and train, then begin our search for recruits. We cannot do this alone; against the vampire we will need help."

For the next twenty years they recruited and trained true believers, developed a network of hunters that stretched out over much of Europe. In all that time they studied, trained, and eliminated a number of hardened criminals, cruel and savage men. Yet, in all that time they never once encountered a true vampire.

Don't miss out!

Visit the website below and you can sign up to receive emails whenever Prudence MacLeod publishes a new book. There's no charge and no obligation.

https://books2read.com/r/B-A-ZKBBB-HDSYC

BOOKS 2 READ

Connecting independent readers to independent writers.

Also by Prudence MacLeod

Children of the Goddess
Lady Blue
Fallen Angel
Lady Justice
Lady Shadow
Lady Seeker
Watcher and Warrior
Shadow Ascending

Children of the Wild
Immortal Tigress
Children of the Wolf
Vampire's Lair
The Hawk and the Wolf
The Oregon Incident
Race the Wind

Forgotten Worlds
Suvi
Echo of the Past

Survivors
Ship
Fleet
Unite
IGEN
T.E.N.

Nova series
Novan Witch
Assassin of Nova
Beyond Nova
Claimstake
Red Nova

Watch for more at https://www.prudencemacleod.com/.

Telling a story is like knitting a sweater. Start with a ball of possibilities, pull out one small thread and begin. With luck patience you will create something quite wonderful.

About the Author

On a far off windswept island Jennifer Crandall sits with her dogs and cats creating fantastic stories for all to enjoy. She publishes as JL Crandall, Prudence MacLeod, and Jenni Leigh.

Read more at https://www.prudencemacleod.com/.